Dougal Henderson has had a bad year. Grieving over the death of his wife and deeply depressed, he is under immense pressure at the Glasgow school where he teaches difficult pupils English. Depressed and struggling with the question of whether life is worth living, he sails the waters off the west coast of Scotland.

Far from finding peace and tranquillity, he is caught in a storm. This he survives, only to become embroiled with drug-smugglers who try to kill him. His yacht is rammed and sunk. Using his stamina and his army training, he outwits the smugglers, discovering in the process a clue that leads him to a bank-note forging operation.

In the company of a new-found friend, Kathleen, Dougal discovers the clandestine printing press. However, the two friends are captured and held prisoner. The pair make their escape but are pursued by ruthless killers across the treacherous marsh-lands that bound the River Spey.

TO DIE OR TO LIVE?

A NOVEL BY
Webster Simpson

TO DIE OR TO LIVE?
© WEBSTER SIMPSON 1999

ISBN 0 9538690-1-6

Published by
Itelsor Ltd
Trendell House
3 Lintrathen Street, Dundee DD5 8EF
Tel: 01382 825629 Fax: 01382 832316

Loch Maree

INVERNESS

The Great Glen

The Cairngorns

Aviemore

Kingussie

Rhum

Eigg

Muck

Tobermory

Oban

Glasgow

Chapter 1

Dougal Henderson stood behind the high-backed wooden chair, gripping it so tightly that his knuckles were white. He looked out at the sea of sullen faces, taking in the mixed emotions on each. For the last school session he had struggled to teach this lot English, despite their resistance to absorbing any kind of education. Dull resentment showed on some faces. Outright boredom could be read on others. A few radiated something between aggression and hatred.

Blackgorge High was a difficult school, or, more precisely, a school grappling with immense difficulties. Its catchment area was the sprawling sixties local authority housing scheme on the eastern outskirts of Glasgow from which it got its name. Every kind of social problem and need was well represented both in the community and in the school. A sexually liberated society provided an endless pool of children to ensure that the school had a long-term future, but almost every child was from a single-parent family or a broken home. In his ten years as an English teacher at Blackgorge, Dougal had learned things that twelve years in the British Army had failed to teach him. Indeed, the Parachute Regiment barracks had been a haven of gentility and culture when compared with Blackgorge High.

The school buildings themselves, a typical product of their era, were no worse, but certainly no better, than the many other poorly designed and shoddily built schools in the vast majority of such deprived areas all over Britain. Dougal had sometimes wondered if there was not a possible doctorate to be won by whoever did a scientific study of the psychological effects of housing children in ugly, damp and dilapidated homes and educating them in equally ugly and poorly maintained schools. If you surrounded a growing body and a developing mind with things of beauty, quality and culture, would the adult of later life be different to the product of a Blackgorge environment? All of Dougal's idealism and enthusiasm which had taken him into teaching after the Falkland's War and his discharge from the paras had gone. Now, on the verge of some kind of breakdown, he was hanging on, but only just.

It had not been a good term. It had not been a good year. This particular Fourth-Year had done nothing to help, but it was not their fault alone. He surreptitiously glanced at his watch. 11.40am. If he could just hold on to his sanity for fifty minutes more, he would survive.

Discipline was on a knife-edge. With term ending and, for most of the class, schooling ending for ever at 12.30pm, there were no sanctions left. It was pointless to threaten even the worst behaved with exclusion from school. So few would find work that they cared nothing about what kind of reference the school might give to a prospective employer. If this lot ganged up on him now, there was little he could do. Ronald Stewart, the tough-looking character in the second row, had set out to make Dougal's life a misery. He had succeeded, probably the only thing he had succeeded in doing in his four years at Blackgorge High. Now his devious face stood out among the others. Dougal gritted his teeth. He started to try to draw out one or two of the more co-operative youngsters in conversation about their holiday plans.

Somehow the remaining fifty minutes passed and, at last, the signal came for his reluctant charges to be released from the bondage of his class for the last time. They streamed out past him. One or two made a friendly remark. Several muttered parting obscenities. He tried to avoid meeting Ronald Stewart's defiant eye, but as he turned away he received a kick in the calf of his right leg. He swung round and only checked himself at the last moment. The temptation to smash that grinning face was nearly overwhelming. It would cost him his career, but it might just be worth it. He turned away. The shuffling of feet receded. At last he was alone.

Dougal sat down behind his big desk and made some pretence at tidying up the sundry papers scattered on it. He could have swept them into the waste-paper bin and left. However, he was deliberately wasting time now. Another ten minutes and the staff room would be empty. He could avoid meeting anyone. He had only to grab his coat and go. How he had managed to hang on until the end of term, he did not know. It was nothing short of miraculous. It was not just the kids, of course. His problems ran so much more deeply than that. Ever since Stella was diagnosed as having an inoperable cancer, he had been living in a twilight world. Watching his wife weaken. Watching her suffer. Watching her die. The experiences of the last eleven months had been shattering. To the world outside, he had presented the traditional stiff upper lip. Inside, he was for ever in tears. To the world outside he was the six foot two ex-soldier whose twelve years in the Army still showed in his military bearing - a strong, confident man whose black hair and beard gave him a striking appearance. Inside, he was on the verge of total collapse.

The last lonely nine weeks had been almost unbearable. He had thrown himself into a regime of constant activity, frightened to be alone, frightened to think. Without the distraction of busyness, his thoughts were so often on ways of ending everything. New and ingenious methods of suicide seemed to grow, uninvited, in his all too vivid imagination. He had told himself that if he could only hang on until the end of term, he would have seven weeks to sort himself out. When the suicidal thoughts came, he pushed them away and instead day-dreamed about sailing out of Oban and off into the stunning scenery of Scotland's rugged west coast.

Now, at last, it could become a reality. A quick visit to home to change, to pick up his gear and he would be off. Dougal had come to hate returning to the empty house. With no Stella, there was only an aching silence. If they had had children, it might have been better. There again, it might have been worse. Both his own and Stella's parents were dead. Perhaps that had made him all the more emotionally dependent on his wife. Now she was gone and he had no one. He must stop thinking obsessively about the past, or he would crack up completely. With an effort of will, he switched his thoughts to Oban, to the Hebrides, those mystic islands off Scotland's western shore. The sooner he was off, the better. He had done most of the necessary packing so, after a quick sandwich and cup of tea, he threw the remaining items of luggage in the boot of his Escort and set off west-wards.

The roads were clear and Dougal accelerated through the glens, over the hills, until he could catch a glimpse of the sun-light reflected on the distant sea-lochs. The road was straight for nearly a mile. He glanced in his mirror. Not a vehicle in sight. Ahead the road swept down equally devoid of traffic. He pressed the accelerator to the floor. 70, 80, 90, 95, 96, 97. The tarmac was swallowed up by the headlong rush of the car. The engine was screaming and the tyres drumming. A sharp bend marked the end of the straight. A sharp bend bounded by a rock-face. How simple to forget to slow down, to forget to turn the wheel. And then to forget everything. The little car hurtled down the slope. The rock-face loomed nearer. He slipped off the buckle of his seat-belt.

Then, in an instant, he had a vision of himself, not finding oblivion and peace in the tangled wreckage of his car, but surviving as a pathetic paraplegic. He slammed on the brakes. The bend loomed up. Somehow, the car made it round the corner, albeit on two wheels. After that he slowed down. The sweat trickled down his face. He was shaking slightly. Was he just a coward? Was he scared of death? No! Firmly he told himself that was not so. When the time was ripe, he would do it, but he would do it properly, with no risk of surviving as the tragic object of everyone's pity.

By the time he reached the fishing haven where his little sloop 'Monica' was moored, the suicidal mood had passed. He parked his car and sat, soaking up the tranquil scene. The tiny bay, almost a mini sea loch itself, was so peaceful. 'Monica', his faithful old yacht, was moored a hundred yards off-shore along with an assortment of pleasure craft and work-boats, each with its twinkling mirror-image. Beyond, on the far shore, he could make out a string of picturesque old cottages and the village pub, set in a frame of Scot's Pines and rhododendrons. The bright purples and pinks stood out beautifully against the rich green back-drop. Immediately behind cows contentedly grazed in the pasture. The fields rose gently until, a mile or so beyond the village, they gave way to, first bracken and scrub, then heather-clad hills that rolled on to the horizon.

Dougal got out of the car, stretched himself, and dragged an inflatable dinghy from the boot. As he pumped it up, an old man who looked as though he must qualify for the post of oldest inhabitant, not merely of the village, but of the whole county, strolled up to him. Dougal turned and his face lit up with pleasure.

"Hello, Angus! My! It's great to see you. How've you been keeping? Man! I envy you, living in a place like this! I see 'Monica's' still afloat, despite all your gloomy predictions!"

"Aye, Dougal, indeed she is." The old man's voice grated

5

like an oil-starved hinge. "I've kept her pumped out for you like we said, but she leaks like a sieve. You really shouldn't be going out in an old tub like that."

Too true, thought Dougal. 'Monica' was one of the first generation of fibre-glass boats and suffered badly from the phenomenon known as 'osmosis'. There were no visible holes in the hull, but she still took in water. The apparently sound, smooth fibre-glass acted like a sponge and the boat slowly but surely filled with water. Only frequent pumping kept her afloat. The truth was that it was only because of this irreparable defect that he had been able to afford to buy her in the first place. He knew she was on her last legs, but she was his, fully paid for.

"Thanks, Angus," he replied. "As long as we keep an eye on the water in the bilges, she'll not go down dramatically. It's not as though I'm often very far from land and I've got the two pumps. Even if the electric one fails, I can keep her dry with the hand one."

"Aye, but it's no just the water seepage. You've no water-tight compartments in that thing. With that great iron keel, she'd go down like a stone."

"She's not as bad as all that! I must admit I do wish she had more buoyancy but the chap who built her reckoned he wanted storage space more than he wanted water-tight compartments." Dougal said.

"Aye, but he was only thinking of sailing on inland waters, not the Atlantic."

"She's sound enough if you keep her pumped out," said Dougal defensively. "A couple of years back, Stella and I were caught out off Staffa in a force six and she was just fine. It was exciting at the time but we were all right. She was always a rather wet boat and we took quite a bit over the bows. However, what with the two pumps and me with a bucket, we survived."

"Well, they do say that the best form of bilge pump is a

frightened man with a bucket! Tell the truth! You were dashed lucky to get off with it! Do you wear a safety harness?"

"Sometimes," replied Dougal rather guiltily. Seldom, would be more truthful.

"Aye, well," said the old man. "You wouldn't know what to do for the best. If a wave washes you overboard, the harness'll save you. If you don't have it on, you can tread water and watch the boat sail herself off to oblivion. On the other hand, if you get pooped by a stern wave, that hulk will go down in seconds and the safety harness'll make sure you go with her. I sometimes think you must have a death-wish, going out into the Minches in that!"

This was getting uncomfortably near the unstated truth. Dougal flushed.

"I'll be fine. Don't you worry. I listen to the shipping forecast and if there's a storm brewing, I find a nice quiet sea-loch and settle down to read and sleep until the blow is over. Anyway, I'd best be getting aboard. I want to sail round to Oban this evening. I'll stock up with supplies there and then I'm off to Tobermory. The forecast is good and I might as well get going while the wind is right."

The old man helped him drag the inflatable down to the water's edge and to load Dougal's kit-bags.

"I'll be away for at least three weeks. I'll give you a phone sometime and let you know what I'm up to. Don't worry if you don't hear from me for a week or so. It all depends on what the wind is like and when I can get to a phone." So saying, he pushed the small craft out into the water and rowed out to the waiting yacht.

'Monica' was a 22 foot sloop. Roughly two-thirds of her length was taken up with the single cabin, leaving an open, self-draining cockpit at the stern. The single mast could carry up to four sails. There was the main sail aft of the mast, two fore-sails and a spinnaker, the latter being the voluminous sail hoisted high on the mast and only used when the wind was very light. Under normal conditions, two sails were adequate, the mainsail plus one fore-sail. The hull could slip through the water at up to eight knots. The boat was very manageable and could be sailed effortlessly into the wind with skilful tacking. Her only weakness was the osmosis. The small cabin smelt of sea-water. Not that that bothered Dougal. The slightly sour smell brought back memories of past holidays, of stormy passages, of halcyon days. He longed to up anchor and head westwards.

It did not take long to transfer the bags from the dinghy to the yacht. He secured the inflatable to the stern and whipped the cover off the little two-cylinder Stuart Turner engine. Old Angus had run up the engine faithfully each week so the battery was fully charged. A push of the button and it throbbed into life. Dougal adjusted the choke and throttle and the engine settled down to a pleasing purr. He clambered forward, passing the mast, and slipped the mooring. The tide gently carried the little boat away from the mooring buoy. By the time Dougal was back at the tiller, the sloop was comfortably clear. He put the engine into gear. The deck below him quivered. The bows rose slightly and the craft, with its dinghy in tow, crept out of the sheltered bay.

The sun was glinting on the water as he rounded the headland. Once clear of the lee of the land, he eased back the throttle and turned the boat so that she was heading directly into the wind. The breeze was such that the mainsail alone would soon carry her to Oban. It was the work of only a couple of minutes to whip the cover off the furled sail that lay along the boom. As he hoisted it, he felt the wind grab the flapping canvas. He slipped back to the cockpit, switched off the engine and pushed the helm over. The rudder progressively gripped the water and the boat's head came round. Like a living thing, the craft heeled gently over before the breeze and started to forge a course through the waves.

Dougal glanced behind. The dinghy was following, riding the water comfortably. The little hamlet receded and he could just make out the bowed form of Angus watching his progress. He raised his arm in a farewell salute and then concentrated on the sea ahead. His cares seemed to slip from him. Already Blackgorge High School seemed a million miles away. Only a dull ache in the calf of his leg reminded him of the obnoxious Ronald Stewart. What was the phrase one of the other teachers had used about that particular brat? "He's got the kind of face you wouldn't tire of kicking!" Really quite apt. With a deliberate effort of will, Dougal pushed the unwelcome memory of the wretch from his mind.

It was still early evening when 'Monica' sailed into Oban bay. Approached from the sea, Oban is an enchanting town. Being the jumping off point for the Hebridean Islands, the pier and ferry-terminal command a significant share of the sea-front. Immediately behind are shops, hotels and a striking cathedral strung around the bay in which Oban nestles. The ground behind rises very steeply and terrace upon terrace of Victorian villas look out across the sound to the island of Kerrera, a mile or so away, and, beyond it, to the more distant hills of Mull. The hill behind these villas is crowned with the magnificent McCaig's Folly, a Victorian piece of gross extravagance, a half-completed replica of Rome's Coliseum. Dougal dropped the sail and nosed in close to the shore near the prominent cathedral. He checked the depth below the keel on the depth-gauge. At two fathoms, he stopped the engine and dropped anchor. The rather excessively large fisherman's anchor was a little unmanageable, but it did ensure that the boat would stay put. He hauled in the dinghy and, with a few strong strokes of the oars, arrived at the steeply-shelving beach. The tide was ebbing, so there was no immediate risk of the tender being washed away.

Nevertheless, he half dragged, half carried it several feet from the water line and secured a rope to a large rock.

It was, of course, mid-summer and the height of the tourist season. It was therefore no surprise for Dougal to find almost every shop still open for business. He did not need much. It was a case of topping up his supplies of milk and bread from a small supermarket and then buying a couple of bottles of whisky and a dozen cans of beer at an off-licence.

Loaded down with his purchases, Dougal headed back to the beach. Ten minutes later, everything was stowed on board. He restarted the engine and raised the anchor. Soon, 'Monica' was purring her way into the setting sun. The harbour at Oban is sheltered from the prevailing westerly winds by the Island of Kerrera. Dougal knew the area well and took the sloop into a sheltered anchorage in the lee of the island. The sun disappeared behind the mass of Kerrera and, although it was not cold, a certain evening chill could be felt in the air. After making sure that the anchor had a good hold, Dougal switched off the engine. A great peace seemed to settle round the vessel. Although there was a slight hum from the traffic in Oban, a mile or so away, the loudest noise was the gentle splash of water as the tide rocked the craft to and fro.

Dougal opened a can and drank deeply. He stretched out his legs across the narrow cockpit and soaked up the tranquillity. Another can, then he began to feel both relaxed and hungry. He stooped and entered the little cabin. In a few moments he had the butane stove hissing gently. To its slight noise was soon added the sizzling of bacon. After bacon, eggs, beans and toast, he began to feel that life was, after all, perhaps worth living. As the shadows of evening gathered around, he poured out half a mug of whisky. He knew he was drinking too much these days, but it was the only way to be sure of something like a good night's sleep. As the whisky started to take effect, he unrolled his sleeping bag. In the growing darkness he lay down and was lulled to sleep by the soft splashing of water and the occasional grumble of the anchor-chain on the shingle bottom below

Chapter 2

The sail up the Sound of Mull was idyllic. Thanks, at least in part, to the whisky, Dougal had slept more soundly than he had for many months. True, he felt a bit stiff, which was hardly surprising as the bunk was both hard and somewhat cramped. However, he felt fine. As he lowered his leg on to the cabin floor, a stab of pain reminded him of school. He rolled up the leg of his jeans. A large multi-coloured bruise was going to remind him of Ronald Stewart for several days to come. He frowned. Teaching had been almost fun when he started. Certainly it seemed much more rewarding than his previous life in the paras. The Falklands had been the turning point. After Goose Green and Bluff Cove, after yomping from San Carlos Bay to Port Stanley, he had imagined he could face anything. Disillusionment had set in quickly, however.

These young thugs were untouchable. Restrain a violent pupil and you will be charged with assault. Brush up against one, boy or girl, in a crowded corridor and it is a sexual assault. Either way, your career is over. Child protection had undoubtedly gone too far. It was only a matter of time before an acute teacher-shortage occurred. The signs were already there. Many of his colleagues would leave the profession at once, given a half-decent offer from commerce or industry. The voluntary sector was already in trouble. Virtually every youth movement in the country was finding it ever harder to recruit volunteer youth leaders.

Dougal rubbed his calf ruefully and, with a deliberate

effort of will, dismissed Ronald Stewart from his thoughts altogether. The wind was somewhere between light and moderate, blowing from the south-west with occasional gusts and turbulence induced by the hills and glens of Mull which was slipping by on the port side. With the main-sail and the larger of the two fore-sails set, 'Monica' sailed smoothly on a north-westerly course so, with the minimum of tacking, Dougal entered Tobermory bay in the middle of the afternoon. Tobermory provides a large sheltered anchorage and, despite its popularity, Dougal found no difficulty in anchoring a hundred yards or so off shore. He rowed ashore and took advantage of the glorious weather to stretch his legs on the hill above the town.

From the hillside, he looked down on the harbour and the many pleasure craft of all sizes moored in the bay. Tobermory itself is a uniquely colourful town with brightly painted buildings along the water-front. Add to that the nearly infinite variety of colours of the yachts and cabin cruisers lying at anchor, then multiply by two to take into account the mirror-image of each reflected in the still waters of the sheltered bay, then place town and bay against the back-drop of the steeply rising hill-side with its greens, purples and browns, and the overall effect is breath-taking. Dougal sat down in the shadow of a larch tree and soaked up the peace of the place.

The following days were sheer pleasure. Despite old Angus and his pessimism, 'Monica' was a joy to sail. True, she leaked, but nothing the pump could not handle. The electric pump had a float-switch and came on automatically if the water built up in the bilges. The wind over the next few days was ideal for sailing, neither too strong nor too light.

A few days later, Dougal decided to leave Tobermory and to head out into the more open water beyond Ardnamurchan Point, the most westerly cape on the British mainland. Beyond that lay the Inner Hebrides, islands, some large and with a substantial population, many scarcely more than reefs with sparse vegetation and both uninhabited and uninhabitable. The shipping forecast was reasonably favourable and he reckoned he could at least reach Mallaig, or possibly even Portree, before the spell of good weather broke.

Before leaving, he telephoned Angus. He did not have to, but there was something vaguely comforting in knowing that someone knew where he was, to the nearest fifty miles or so. Since Stella died, he had totally lost contact with his two cousins, his only living relatives. The solitary life suited him, but just once in a while, he wished someone cared whether he lived or died.

"You watch yourself in that plastic basin of a boat," the old man said in his usual rasping tone. "You'll have no chance in anything like a heavy sea. That thing was built for the Norfolk Broads, not the Atlantic."

"All right, all right," replied Dougal wearily. He knew perfectly well Angus was right, but still felt a sense of personal injury every time 'Monica' was criticised. "I'll take care. The way you talk, anyone would think you expected her to break up if I sneeze violently! She's old, but she's mine and she's paid for!"

"There's no telling you, is there? One of these days, she'll sink like a stone and carry you to perdition with her."

"Now! Now! That's hardly language becoming of an elder of the Kirk. I thought you believed in a better life hereafter? You make it sound as though death was the worst thing that could befall a fellow!"

"Depends if you know where you're bound for hereafter," was the enigmatic reply.

Dougal did not want to be drawn into a theological debate, still less to be at the receiving end of a sermon. "Don't you worry! I'll be careful. I'll give you a ring from Skye. It depends on the wind, but I've supplies for at least a week. If it starts to blow, I'll lie up in a sheltered loch for as long as it takes"

They exchanged the usual farewells and he hung up. The old man's comment, "Depends if you know where you're bound for hereafter," echoed in his mind. "To be, or not to be? That is the question." The words from Shakespeare's 'Hamlet' surfaced in his head. In some ways he, Dougal, was struggling with the same dilemma as Hamlet. Was life worth living, or should he end it all? Hamlet had been deterred from suicide by the fear of something after death. Was that same fear what had kept Dougal from slamming the car into the rock-face? He thought not, but was not altogether sure. Old Angus was sure, quietly trusting his God for this life and a future one and Dougal found himself envying his friend's confidence. He decided he would not rush into a decision, but sooner or later he would have to decide quite rationally whether to die or to live.

Leaving the telephone box, he set out on a last trip to stock up on what he thought of as luxuries, like eggs, bacon, milk and bread, at the same time buying essentials like whisky and beer. Dougal then rowed out to the waiting yacht. He stowed all the provisions and deflated the dinghy. It would be some days before he would need it again and, in the relatively open seas beyond Ardnamurchan, the little tender might easily be swamped if he towed it. At last, all was ship-shape and he pulled up the anchor, lashing it down on the tiny fore-deck. Half a mile later, in the mouth of Tobermory Bay, he cut the engine, hoisted the sails and headed westwards. Ardnamurchan Point, with its lighthouse, crept by on the starboard side.

The heat haze was already exaggerating distances and soon the mainland slipped astern, becoming scarcely more than a smudge on the horizon. Ahead, in the distance, Dougal could just see the outline of Coll. Although the distance was not great, with his eye-level only some four feet from the water, the curvature of the earth restricted his visibility considerably. This did not bother Dougal. With compass, chart and depth-sounder, he felt totally confident of getting to where he wanted, even if a sea mist cut his vision completely. Leaving Ardnamurchan well away to the starboard, he set a new course, more or less due north. By early afternoon, those quaintly named islands of the Inner Hebrides, first Muck, then Eigg, then Rhum, crawled over the horizon. Rather than press on to Mallaig, Dougal decided to spend the night in the sheltered anchorage at Arisaig.

Chapter 3

Dougal did not bother going ashore, but settled down after his evening meal with a book, a bottle of Scotch and a few cans of beer. Perhaps this affected his judgement, for he missed the shipping forecast. Thanks to the alcohol, he spent what might be described as an increasingly mellow evening followed by a deep night's sleep. The price was a first-class hang-over. The wind had fallen away during the night and Dougal used the engine to get 'Monica' well out into open water before he hoisted sail. There was hardly any wind and the morning passed with very little real progress. The heat-haze built up as the day progressed and both the mainland and the various islands virtually disappeared. Soon after noon, the wind came away in gusts. If Dougal had been more on the ball, he would have recognised the signs of an approaching storm. If he had heard and heeded the gale warnings which had preceded the main shipping forecast, he would never have left Arisaig.

The first serious gusts struck from the south-east in mid-afternoon. Dougal quicky dropped the mainsail. Even so, the small craft lurched alarmingly as the wind caught the fore-sail. Working as quickly as he could, he replaced the large fore-sail with the smallest of his storm-sails, a mere triangular rag of a thing, but enough to give the craft some steerage way and some stability. The wind force strengthened. It was at least force four, with gusts that had to be force six or perhaps even seven. With the wind, came squalls of torrential rain. Lashing the tiller, Dougal hastily pulled a dry-suit over his clothes. 'Monica' was a wet boat at the best of times, but she was shipping water over the bows at an alarming rate. The electric pump was working continuously and, holding the tiller firmly in his right hand, Dougal operated the hand-pump feverishly with his left.

All thought of navigation was gone now. The yacht ran before the wind. The wind direction was almost straight from the east now. Dougal peered through the rain and the sea-spray. The last thing he wanted was to come up on a lee shore. He was not sure where Rhum was. Somewhere to the south, he hoped. Neither did he know where Skye was. Somewhere to the north, with any luck. 'Monica' was making heavy weather of it but Dougal was not too worried about her foundering in the open sea. Being cast up on a lee shore was a different proposition and one that he dreaded. He glanced at his watch. It was only just after five, yet, with the heavy cloud and driving rain, it was almost dark. All he could do was to let her run before the wind and hope that she would not be pooped by some huge sea. He looked anxiously over his shoulder. Roller after roller towered up behind the boat. Each one looked as though it would crash its tons of green water on her, but each one lifted the stern and passed harmlessly underneath.

The storm continued unabated into the night. Dougal eventually concluded that the immediate risk of fetching up on one of the islands was over. He must have passed safely through the Cuillin Sound and by now be safe in the open waters of the Sea of the Hebrides. The truth was he did not know where he was. The Outer Hebrides must be dead ahead, but safely thirty or more miles away. Surely the storm would blow itself out before he reached there. Somewhere to the north was the north-west tip of Skye, but that should be at least ten miles off his starboard bow. 'Monica' would not let him down. She would ride it out.

Time slipped by, but the storm showed no sign of abating.

It was pitch dark by nine, but Dougal did not dare leave the tiller to switch on the riding lights. Perhaps it did not matter. The chances of encountering any other vessel were remote. The mast-head light might be seen by a ship with an alert look-out, but the port and starboard ones would be under the water almost as often as they were above it. His arm ached mercilessly with the persistent pumping, but he had to keep going. The electric pump alone would be fighting a losing battle.

As the night wore on, with the storm still raging, his aches and pains increased. In a weird flash-back, he remembered the car hurtling down the long straight, the nearly overwhelming impulse to hold it steady until it smashed into the fast-approaching rock-face. He remembered releasing the seat-belt. Why, he found himself asking, why was he making such an effort to hang on to his unwanted life now? All he had to do was to stop pumping. A few swigs from the whisky bottle would help add a touch of unreality to the whole business. Why, then, bother struggling to survive? "To be, or not to be? That is the question." To die or to live? Why, despite his misery, did he cling with such tenacity to life? He found no answer. Only a vague feeling that one day he would decide to die - but not quite yet.

With the dawn came a slight moderating of the wind, although the rain still fell in unrelenting torrents. With the slackening of the wind came sufficient easing of the waves to allow him to stop pumping. The electric pump could cope now. He lashed the tiller and stretched himself stiffly. Opening the cabin, he reached inside rather than entered and grabbed half a loaf of bread, a chunk of cheddar and several chocolate bars. These, together with a couple of cans of export, he rammed inside the front of his dry-suit. As he turned, a squall hit the boat, she lurched and Dougal only just managed to grab the tiller in time to prevent himself going over the side. As it was, a large sea surged over him, flooding the cockpit. He grabbed the pump and worked like fury until, at last, the situation was under control. It was all too clear that he was not out of danger yet and that it would be many hours before he could relax.

Fearing the electric pump would drain the battery, Dougal ran up the engine. He set it to run in neutral at a fast enough tick-over to put a charge in the battery without using more fuel than was necessary. This was not because of penny-pinching. Having no idea how far he was from land, Dougal had no means of knowing how much petrol he might go through before he could refuel.

For all that he was sitting in damp clothes, the cold did not trouble him. It was, after all, still mid-summer and the air temperature was not unseasonably low, even in spite the continuous rain. Apart from that, the dry-suit, with its thick neoprene to insulate his body, enfolded him in a clammy warmth. Gratefully, Dougal tore lumps out of the half-loaf and munched this together with mouthfuls of cheese. With some difficulty, he opened a can of beer using only one hand as the other held the tiller. Whilst he would much rather have had tea, he was desperately thirsty and glad of any kind of drink.

Throughout the day, the wind lessened. The rain, too, was less persistent. Visibility was still poor, with spume being whipped off the creaming waves. Cautiously he stood up. His eyes swept his limited horizon. Nothing to be seen but the white-topped waves. The wind was still blowing from the east, but had now moderated to a degree where Dougal felt he could risk tacking into it. He swung the helm to starboard. The boat came round to lie abeam the wind. He let out the storm-sail and the wind caught it. 'Monica' heeled over sharply, dipping her bows deeply into a wave. He pulled the sail in tight and the boat started to make headway in a north-easterly direction.

The fact that he was utterly lost did not really worry

Dougal. He was somewhere in the Minches. Westwards must lie the Outer Hebrides, always assuming he had not been driven so far south or so far north that a westward course would have him sailing out into the Atlantic, with the next stop Canada. This was highly unlikely. The chances were that he was only a few miles off the Outer Hebrides. Going there had few attractions, however. The wind might have moderated, but it was still a frightening thought to be driven by it on to a lee shore. True, he had the engine and some reserve of fuel, but, against both wind and current, the little Stuart Turner might simply not have enough power. Heading east, even though it was into the wind, was a safer option. If he went east, he must reach either one of the Inner Hebrides or the mainland. However far he might have been blown, Scotland was too big a target to miss. Furthermore, if the wind persisted in the east, whilst tacking against it would undoubtedly be laborious, it was bound to slacken as he came under the shelter of the shore.

Towards evening, the wind fell away to a gentle breeze. The seas were still running high, but gave no cause for anxiety. Dougal lashed the helm and made his way cautiously forward. He dropped the storm-sail and put out a sea anchor. 'Monica' swung round with her bows to waves and settled down to a comfortable fore and aft pitch. Dougal staggered into the cabin. He began to realise just how tired he was. The boat was still rolling too much for him to attempt to make tea, or indeed, to cook anything. He ate more bread and more chocolate, washing it down with a little beer diluted with a lot of whisky. Then he made sure the boats riding lights were on and gratefully tumbled, still fully dressed, into his bunk. Within seconds he was sound asleep.

Chapter 4

When Dougal woke up, the storm had very clearly blown itself out. There was still a heavy swell, but now long rolling waves instead of the creaming vicious ones of the previous day. 'Monica' rose and fell gently. The wind had dropped to virtually nothing. The barometer had started to rise, so Dougal felt reasonably sure that the worst was over and that he was not just in the eye of the storm. He looked at his watch. My! He must have been tired! It was not far short of mid-day. Not that that mattered. There was so little wind that, even if he had hoisted sail at first light, he would only have moved a mile or two.

Certain that the weather was set to remain calm, Dougal concentrated on eating. He was soon drinking his first hot drink for over forty eight hours. Sausage, bacon and eggs were simmering in the pan and he was feeling ravenous. There was no particular hurry. The wind might freshen in the afternoon, in which case he would head east. If it didn't, it would not matter if he stayed becalmed for a day or two. He had ample supplies. The boat's bilges were pumped dry. It did not bother him that he was out of sight of land and totally unsure of his position. The worst was undoubtedly past and 'Monica' had not let him down. So much for Angus and his gloomy prophecies!

Everything in the boat was wet. Although the cabin door had ensured that, even when the waves swamped the cockpit, they went no farther, the spray which had enveloped the sloop during the storm had penetrated everywhere. As the sun struggled out from behind the patchy cloud, Dougal strung out his spare clothes and his sleeping bag to dry on the cabin roof. If he had had any dry clothes, he would have changed. As it was, by the time the gear on the cabin had dried, so had that on his back and he therefore did not bother to change. After all, there was no one in the middle of the Minch to see or to smell him!

It was late afternoon before the wind rose sufficiently to make it worth hoisting sail. He re-packed his now dry spare clothes and replaced the storm-sail with the larger of his two fore-sails. He then hoisted the main-sail. 'Monica' heeled gently over and started to respond slowly to the helm. He tacked into the wind in a north-easterly direction. It would be interesting to see how long it took him to sight land and whether that land would be the Island of Skye or the mainland beyond it.

As the evening progressed, Dougal tacked to and fro, first north-east, then south-east. 'Monica' was clipping along at six or seven knots, but, with the need to keep tacking, progress towards land was probably only a couple of miles in each hour. That did not matter. The weather was fine and, if night overtook him, he would stop sailing and put out a sea-anchor for the few hours of total darkness. He would be able to be on the move again by 3am or thereabouts. This far north, it did not really get completely dark in mid-summer, provided the skies were clear. However, with the patchy cloud following the storm, it would almost certainly be necessary to stop for two or three hours.

Just before mid-night, the wind fell away and the skies clouded over. Dougal furled the sails and put out the sea-anchor. 'Monica' swung lazily on the anchor rope, heaving gently on the slight swell. As he was not yet tired enough to sleep, Dougal settled down to have a large and leisurely supper. An hour later, feeling well-fed and well-satisfied, he lounged back in the cockpit and opened his third can of beer.

The moon appeared from time to time, glinting on the water. Most of the time, however, it disappeared behind the slow-moving cloud. At times, in the moon-light, Dougal thought he could make out the dark shape of land to the north. If it were, it was too far off to cause any anxiety and it would still be there in the morning. Investigation could wait. The darkness, when the moon was obscured, was almost complete, broken only by the green reflection and the red reflection, on starboard and port sides respectively, of the riding lights. Aloft, the white mast-head light shone out brightly, although it cast but little light downwards. The atmosphere was very much that of the calm after the storm.

A couple of hours or so later, Dougal was dozing contentedly, when he was aroused by the distant throb of an engine. The night was by now both dark and still. The noise became louder. He stood up and peered out into the night. He could see nothing. The engine was that of a fairly large craft, with that pulsating tone that was characteristic of twin diesels. Still he could see nothing. He had no difficulty placing the noise. It was almost abeam of him on the starboard side and it was getting alarmingly close. He grabbed his butane operated foghorn and gave a long blast. Even if the helmsman on the approaching craft were dozing, that should waken him. Still the volume increased. Then he saw, first the phosphorescence from the bow wave, then the dark shape of a black hull bearing down on him. He jabbed the starter of the engine and blasted his foghorn again. The engine fired instantly. He thrust it into gear and rammed the throttle wide open. The gap between the two vessels was only yards and was closing fast. 'Monica' surged forward and the black hull crashed past, missing her stern by less than two yards. For about fifty yards, the little sloop slipped through the water, over-running her sea-anchor. Then the engine coughed, spluttered and stopped. Dougal knew immediately what

had happened. The anchor's rope had fouled the propeller. 'Monica' now lay dead in the water.

Dougal was furious. The other craft carried no lights and, with difficulty, he spotted it. It was difficult to identify what kind of ship it was. Probably a sea-going tug or something of that sort. It was a fair size, all of seventy feet, he guessed. The silhouette of the boat could be seen as it made a tight turn only a couple of hundred yards or so away. The moon chose this moment to break hazily through the cloud.

The tug, or whatever it was, now had completed the turn and was pounding down on the stricken 'Monica'. There was no room for doubt. He was going to be rammed and there was nothing he could do about it.

When the advancing craft was only thirty yards away, Dougal took a deep breath and dived over the stern. Once in the water, he went deep. Overhead he could hear the roar of the twin propellers. What they would do to a human body did not bear thinking about. However, by the time they passed over and the noise started to recede, he was at least thirty feet down. Conserving his energy, he swam with long, slow strokes on the reverse of the course of the rogue boat, rising gently towards the surface. The moonlight gave him but a second or so's warning that he was about to break surface. He stopped swimming and pulled the hood of his dry-suit over his head. With scarcely a ripple, his head emerged and he gulped down lung-fulls of blessed fresh air. Then he turned cautiously towards where 'Monica' had been. She had, as Angus had predicted, gone down like a stone. The tug was turning again. The noise of her engines fell away and she closed the gap between her and the swimmer.

Dougal had often thought of shaving off his beard. He had been quite proud of it when it was jet black. Now that it was lightly streaked with grey, he had begun to feel it added to his age and did nothing for his looks. However, he was glad of it that night. He pulled the hood down to his eyes and kept his face down, peering through his eye-brows. A searchlight came on and a great shaft of white light swept the water. Dougal did a noiseless duck-dive and swam strongly away from the ship. When his lungs felt they were bursting, he surfaced again. He had put another sixty yards between himself and the searchlight. A dark figure on the bows hooked something out of the water, Dougal's life-jacket, probably the only thing left afloat from his sloop.

Dougal was absolutely sure that the rogue ship was not trying to rescue survivors and, much as he disliked the idea of being adrift in the deep, he was relieved when, eventually, the searchlight was doused, the heavy diesels burst into life and the darkened ship disappeared. Relieved he might be, but as Dougal surveyed his extremely limited horizon, the awful reality of being alone in these waters came home to him. When your eye-level is only three or four inches above the surface, you do not see very far. In near total darkness, you hardly see at all. The sea was practically a flat calm now, although the long, low, rolling waves lifted him at regular intervals. Somewhere, in a pocket under the dry-suit, he knew he had a pocket compass. The boat's compass, of course, had, like everything else, gone down with 'Monica'. He tried to pull out the compass, but he soon concluded that, short of getting out of the dry-suit, he could not reach it.

So far as he could remember from his para days, survival time in the sea was dependent on temperature and clothing. Whether he swam or tried to conserve his strength would not make much difference. Swimming seemed a bit pointless when he had no idea where to swim to. While all these thoughts were swirling round his mind, the moon came out from behind the clouds. He raised himself as high as he could and looked all round. Dimly he could discern the dark mass of the land that he had noticed earlier. However, now it was much closer and he realised that he was being swept in its general direction by quite a strong current. Dougal started swimming, using a long, slow breast-stroke that he felt he could keep up indefinitely.

Half an hour later, the dark mass of the land was much nearer. He guessed it was one of the dozens of small islands that made up the Hebrides. He also perceived that the current was carrying him past it. As it slipped by on his left, he put all he had into his swimming. Just when it seemed he would be swept on past it, a back-water swung him round into the lee of the island. There the ground rose steeply and, as he approached, the bulk of the island came between him and the moon. One minute it was clearly silouhetted, then it disappeared and he was in a pool of black shadow. He swam towards it and suddenly his foot struck a reef. He tried to stand, but his feet slithered on the slimy seaweeds. Sometimes crawling, sometimes swimming, he struggled past the outcrops of rock until he was at last on a shingle beach.

For several minutes, he just sat, glad to feel solid ground under him. Then he climbed up the foreshore and, groping in the darkness, scrambled up the steeply sloping, windswept turf above. It took only minutes to reach the top and there he sank down to the ground once more. Emerging from the dark side of the island into the moonlight felt as though someone had put a light on.

From this vantage point, Dougal could see that the island was small. It was obviously a long narrow reef, big enough to have vegetation, but too small to be inhabited. It's breadth, at the widest point, was only a couple of hundred yards. How long it was, he was not sure. His view along the spine of the island was cut off by a high spur of rock. Cautiously he made his way along the ridge. He rounded the spur and looked down a steep descent to a narrow inlet. Anchored a hundred yards off shore, was the sinister shape of the ship that had run 'Monica' down. A rowing boat was pulled up on the shore and three men were unloading packages from it and concealing them behind some rocks. Dougal obviously had not been spotted even though he must have been clearly visible on the skyline. He knew that the human eye could detect sudden movement in twilight conditions so he sank very slowly to his knees and then lay flat.

Suddenly it was like the Falklands all over again - the same inhospitable terrain, the same tension as he had experienced then, wondering if Argentinean eyes were following his every movement. The men below carried on with their work without looking up. If there was anyone on the ship, he clearly had not spotted Dougal. There could be little doubt as to what he had stumbled on. Dougal knew that the hundreds of miles of the rugged Scottish west coast was the entry point for most of Britain's illicit drugs. He had had the misfortune to fall foul of an unscrupulous gang of smugglers. The occasional word floated up the hill to where he lay. It was not Spanish or French. He had a working knowledge of both. It might be German or, perhaps, Dutch. He could not be sure.

When the boat had made another trip out to the mother craft and back, it became clear that landing the cargo was finished. The three men rowed off again and soon the anchor was raised and the ship, still with no lights, pulled away from the island. The moon disappeared behind the cloud and Dougal lay prone in the darkness. While all the tension was there, he had hardly been aware of his discomforts. Now, the cold seemed to penetrate to his very marrow. He staggered stiffly to his feet and picked his way down to the bay. The cargo was concealed and a casual passer-by would not have noticed it, not that many casually passed by this spot. Under a dark green tarpaulin was a pile of brown packages. Dougal sat back on his heels, deep in thought. Obviously, someone would come to transfer the cargo to the mainland. Whoever that was would be every bit as ruthless as the foreigners. He badly needed to rescued, but not by drug-smugglers.

Dougal shivered. He must find shelter and try to generate some heat. He had the butane cigarette-lighter that he always carried with him on the yacht. He was not a smoker, but trying to light the stove with damp matches had taught him the value of the cigarette-lighter years ago. However, dare he light a fire? There was all the fuel he needed scattered as driftwood along the tide-line. He returned to the high spur of rock and looked all round. It was still very dark, but the sky was lightening in what he guessed was the north-east. Dawn would be only an hour or so away. To the south-east, there was a slight orange glow in the sky, reflecting on the clouds. It was so slight that he might be imagining it. Alternatively, it could be the glow of street lights in some distant village. As the glow of dawn increased in the sky, he could see a little more of the northern side. There was no sign of land and no sign of boats, only the unbroken expanse of the sea. If he were to light a fire, that would be the place to do it.

Scrambling down the slope, Dougal reached the shore at a small cove flanked by cliffs rising twenty or so feet. In the lee of one of these, he lit two small fires, about six feet apart. The damp wood put out some smoke initially, but as the fires took, only a faint blue haze drifted upwards. By the time it reached the top of the island, it would surely be so dispersed as to be invisible. Standing between the two fires, Dougal stripped off all his clothes. He laid them out systematically on the rocks to dry whilst he soaked up the heat of the fires. An hour or so later the sun rose above the sea to the east, its early morning rays just reaching into the north-facing bay. There was, as yet, no heat in the sunlight, but the psychological effect was good. He started to feel hungry. Thank goodness he had eaten so heartily yesterday evening! It would be long enough before he could hope to eat again. Thirst was going to be an even greater problem. The island was too small to support any streams and the one or two natural depressions which had collected rain water were clearly polluted by seagull droppings. With an effort of will, Dougal stopped thinking about food and drink.

As soon as his clothes were dry, he hurriedly dressed. A man feels terribly vulnerable with nothing on! It was warm enough now to do without the dry-suit. He had been grateful for it, and its insulation may well have saved his life, but he was glad to be free of its clammy embrace. He squatted down between the fires, enjoying the sensation of being almost too warm. Why did he feel so glad he had been wearing the dry-suit? Without its neoprene warmth, he might have been comfortably dead by now. He thought again of the suicidal thoughts that had filled his mind in recent months.

Eventually he decided he just did not understand himself at all. He had dreamed of welcoming, indeed, of inviting, death, but when he had the chance to die, he fought tooth and nail against it.

He was frankly baffled.

As the sun rose, Dougal let the two fires die down. Someone would come to pick up the drugs, but his gut feeling was that it would be under cover of darkness. However, it would be safer to seek a suitable hiding place and to stay well out of sight. He climbed up to the top of the ridge, crawling the last few yards to ensure that he would not be seen against the skyline. Lying flat in the grass, he carefully surveyed the whole view to the south and east. A light sea mist hung a few feet above the water. Over it, to the south-east, he could see a distant shore. The mist distorted the view and made judging distances very difficult. Perhaps eight or ten miles, he reckoned. In the far distance to the south was a biggish vessel heading west. Probably a Caledonian McBrayne ferry outward bound for Lewis. Apart from that, there was nothing visible, although a small craft could be lurking in the mist. Dougal slid down a few feet and cautiously scanned the north and west. Again a mist and, this time no sign of either land or ships. He decided to return to the inlet where the drugs lay.

There were two reefs of rock bounding the inlet, forming a natural harbour. The tide was coming in and Dougal guessed high tide would be at about noon. This meant that the cargo would either be uplifted at noon, or, more likely, at midnight. Beyond the pile of drugs, Dougal scrambled up the steeply sloping ground above it. On the far side, it dropped steeply into a small cove, bounded by sheer rocks some thirty feet high. The cove was virtually inaccessible from the land without a rope. If the packets containing the drugs were dropped over the edge, they would land so close to the cliff as to be almost impossible to see from above. If the pick-up was not made at noon, he could, with very little effort, magic the whole lot away before midnight. He did consider the simpler course of dumping the stuff in the sea, but he instinctively wanted to keep the evidence handy in the hopes that the drug-runners might somehow be brought to justice. There being little else he could do until it was clear that the smugglers were not coming at noon, he made his way to the other end of the island. There he found a deep hollow on the southern side which was a natural sun-trap. When he lay down in it, he was completely hidden from the seaward side and would only be discovered if someone walked very close to the spot. He lay down in the sun and was soon asleep.

Chapter 5

It was late afternoon before Dougal awoke, feeling refreshed, but very hungry. There was nothing he could do about that. He had been trained in survival, but it was hard to imagine anyone could survive for long on this apology for an island. He pushed thoughts of food from his mind and climbed to the top of the ridge. Careful not to show himself against the skyline, he looked round in every direction. The mist had lifted and visibility was excellent. Both to the north and the south, he could make out distant vessels of some sort or other, probably fishing or lobster boats. All were impossibly far out of signalling range. To the west was open sea. To the east, perhaps ten miles away, was the line of the coast. By now, Dougal felt sure it was the coast of the Scottish mainland, rather than of some outlying island.

The tide was nearly fully out and he returned to the inlet where the drug haul lay. As he had expected, it was untouched. The pick-up time must be mid-night. The two projecting reefs which ran thirty yards or so out into the water with a twenty yard gap between formed a natural harbour. Dougal walked down the shingle between them and examined the rocks. On the left-hand one he detected smudges of paint. Obviously, someone had moored a boat against the rock at high tide and that must have been fairly recently. There was no sign of paint on the other side and, as the side of the reef there was much more jagged, Dougal was sure that anyone who knew the inlet would choose the left-hand side.

The reef there was covered in black sea-weed up to the high-tide mark. Above that, was smooth, bare rock which rose gently and eventually disappeared under the sparse but hardy vegetation of the island.

A stone's throw from the edge of the reef, Dougal found a depression in the ground that, with very little adaptation, would conceal him. An idea was forming in his mind. The inlet could not accommodate a very big boat. Therefore he could expect something less than thirty foot, most probably an open fishing boat whose activities in the Minch even at night would not arouse suspicion. A boat that size would suggest a maximum crew of four. If they could be drawn away from the boat, he might just be able to sneak round behind them, steal it and leave them stranded. Provided there was only one man left with the boat, Dougal, with his unarmed combat training, ought to be able to neutralise him.

Dougal climbed up the ridge again. There was still no sign of any boat within five miles of the island. He had not expected to see one, the tide being so far out, but it was better to be safe. He returned to the inlet and, for half an hour, toiled at carrying packets up the slope and dropping them carefully down the cliff. The care was not out of consideration for the drugs, but to ensure that they landed as close to the cliff as possible and were therefore almost invisible from above. He reckoned that the half hour had accounted for about a quarter of the packages, perhaps two hundred kilos or so. He scaled the ridge and looked around. Nothing had changed. He returned to the inlet and worked another half hour stint. Once more, he checked the seas round the island. Still all clear. He repeated this procedure until all but two packets had been dumped.

Dougal then took the two and carried them up the ridge. About half way up, he carefully dropped one, gashing a tear in it along a jagged outcrop of rock. A stream of white pills flowed through the rent in the plastic. Dougal knew little about drugs, but guessed these were 'Ecstasy' tablets. He carefully spread them out, so that, although they still looked as though they had been accidentally spilt, they covered a wide area and would be visible against the dark ground, even in bad light. He carried the second bag over the top and some distance along the ridge. There, he made another spillage. The plastic bag itself he carried on a farther fifty yards and then left it several feet down the south side of the ridge, hoping that this would suggest that the main haul had been taken back down to sea-level at that point. He looked at his watch. Just after nine. It was unlikely that any one would come for at least a couple of hours but, to be safe, he returned to the inlet and settled down in the hollow to wait, trying not to think about his growing hunger and even more serious thirst. If the pick-up party did not come tonight, tomorrow would not be pleasant.

The evening passed slowly. The sun sank in the north-west, lighting the distant streamers of cloud with rich reds, oranges and yellows. Just before eleven, Dougal heard the sound of an engine, very distant at first, but growing stronger by the moment. With infinite care, he peered out from his hiding place. An open boat was nosing into the inlet. The engine was shut down to a tick-over and he could hear low voices, too low and too distant for him to make out what was being said. The light was failing fast, but looking up the ridge, he was gratified to see the white trail of tablets looking almost fluorescent in the gloaming.

How many men. One, two , three. Any more? No. Three it was! The boat came alongside and one jumped out with a rope which he quickly attached to a large rock. The engine was switched off and the other two scrambled ashore. The three were now only yards away from where Dougal lay in the depression in the ground. Suddenly, it seemed a most inadequate hiding place. If they found him and, assuming they were as murderous as the gang of the previous night, he had had it. However, they scarcely looked round, but strode over to where Dougal had left the tarpaulin. They whipped it aside and their excited and angry voices told him they had discovered their loss. Now everything depended on them not doing a systematic sweep from one end of the island to the other. If they did, they could hardly fail to find him. One of the men moved in his direction. Any closer and he would see Dougal's prostrate form. Dougal pressed himself to the ground, not daring to move a muscle.

Suddenly a cry told him that the spilt tablets had been spotted. All three took the bait and rushed up the ridge. One of them climbed to the top. He shouted to the others. They all dashed up and over the top. The moment they disappeared, Dougal was on his feet. He sprinted over to the boat, untied the rope and, seizing an oar, punted it backwards out to open water. There, he started to row. It was a big and rather clumsy boat for one man to handle, but Dougal wanted to put some distance between himself and the island before he tried to start an unfamiliar engine. These men were crooks and, if caught, would get a heavy gaol sentence. They would be ruthless. They might be armed.

Two hundred yards from the island, Dougal shipped the oars. His presence was still undetected and he was far enough out to try the engine. If the three on the island were armed, it could only be with hand-guns. Dougal himself had been rated quite well as a marksman, but knew that, in the poor light, he would have been unable to be sure of a hit at this range. At worst, these would be enthusiastic amateurs, not trained marksmen. He need not worry.

The engine was an inboard petrol one and Dougal struggled to see how to start it. The daylight was practically gone and there was enough breeze to keep on blowing out his cigarette lighter. However, he soon worked out the controls and the engine roared into life. Its throb was obviously heard on the island. There were angry shouts and the crack of a pistol. Keeping his head down, Dougal steered, first south, then east. He took a bearing with his pocket compass, which was just as well, because, as he neared the land, the darkness deepened. The orange glow he had fancied he saw the previous night, became clearer as he progressed. No doubt there was a village, but would it be wise to seek out a harbour there? It was probably the home port of whoever he had marooned on the island. As it was now midnight, anyone up and about might be associated with the drug-running. Gone were the days when a remote highland village would have its own police-house and policeman. The nearest police station might be forty miles away.

As he neared the shore, Dougal cut the throttle back and the engine note dropped to a barely audible burple. The street lights were now visible, a single line of them a hundred yards or so long. The indications were that this would be a cluster of houses strung out along a single road. Cautiously, Dougal nosed the boat into a cove about half a mile north of the village. He cut the engine and let the bows run aground. Without pausing to moor it, he leapt ashore and hurried up the beach to the shelter of some scrubby bushes. There, he paused. There was not a sound, save the gentle murmur of the surf on the shingle. He moved inland and soon found himself on a single-track tarmac road. To the south he could now see the street lights. To the north was the dark mass of a building a hundred yards away. Keeping very quiet, he approached it. It was in total darkness and towered over the road, being itself high and also built at the top of a steep slope. When he was able to pick out the shape of it against the night-sky, he realised it was the parish church, standing in the midst of a small grave-yard. Beyond it was an imposing stone-built house which had to be the manse. Not for the first time, Dougal wondered why the Church of Scotland, unlike its English counterpart which placed churches in the centre of communities, often built them at the edge of a village. However, its relative isolation suited him now.

There was a light on in the manse, for which Dougal was glad. He did not like the idea of rousing a minister from his bed and trying to persuade him to believe his unlikely tale. He rang the door-bell. After a slight delay, the door was opened to reveal a middle-aged man, casually dressed, slightly stooped and balding.

"I'm sorry to knock you up at this time of night," said Dougal. "I've had a brush with drug-smugglers and I must contact the police."

The man looked startled, which was hardly surprising. The West Highlands have a minimal crime rate and the notion of drug-runners in his parish would come as a shock to any minister.

"You'd better come in and tell me more," the man replied. His accent was more Glasgow than the soft lilt of the Highlands. "Come through to the kitchen. I've just made tea. Come and have a cup and let me hear your story."

Dougal would have liked to have phoned the police first but he was hungry and thirsty. The men on the island were not going anywhere. They could wait. He was followed his host into a large farmhouse-style kitchen.

"Milk? Sugar? His host asked. "Biscuits? Or would you like something more substantial."

"I've not eaten for over twenty-four hours. A chunk of bread and butter would be lovely if you can spare it." The other rapidly spread four or five thick slabs of bread and set them down before Dougal along with a selection of jam and a steaming mug of tea. As he munched the bread gratefuly, Dougal summarised the events of the last couple of days as briefly as he could.

"So you marooned them on the island! Smart move that. We must phone the police." The man rose to his feet. "You say you hid the drugs. Where did you put them? I should have thought there could not be many hiding places on a small island like that." As Dougal explained about dropping them over the cliff, the other man moved to the door.

"I'll see about phoning, then," he said. "What did you say your name was?"

Dougal had not. Some instinct told him to try to remain anonymous. Even if he emerged a hero, it could never look good to have any reference to drugs on his CV. People never remembered things accurately. In a year or two's time staff room conversations would go something like "Henderson? Yes, I remember him. Got mixed up in drug-smuggling, didn't he? Must have wriggled off the hook somehow if he's still teaching. Probably could afford a crack lawyer. Profits on drugs are enormous, you know." Apart from that, even if the smugglers were imprisoned, they would have friends outside.

"Stewart," he said. "Ronald Stewart."

The man opened a large cupboard, reached in and then swung round and pointed a large shot-gun at Dougal's chest.

"My friends are not going to be best pleased at you for leaving them on the island. On your feet! Over to the door!" He pointed to a door at the back of the kitchen. "Open it. Outside! This gun's six inches from your spine. One false move and you'll have a hole the size of a football in your guts."

He picked a large key off a hook on the door-frame and followed Dougal outside. Dougal knew enough about gunshot wounds to give the fellow no excuse to pull the trigger. He was prodded in the back with the shotgun barrel and steered up a pathway to the rear of the house. The ground ahead rose steeply to the wall that bounded the graveyard some forty feet away. There was no chance of escape. To try would be suicide. Suicide! That word again! He had thought of it so often. Now death was only seconds away if he cared to choose it. A wave of anger surged through him. No one else was going to decide the "How? Where? When?" of his death. He obediently walked up the path. At the corner of the building, the man with the gun stepped on to the grass so he could keep Dougal covered as he rounded the corner. A few yards beyond was a heavy door securely closed with a substantial batten of wood wedging it shut.

"Open it!" grunted his captor, passing Dougal the key. Having no practical alternative, he did so. He was abruptly pushed inside and the door slammed shut.

"You can stay there until the others decide what to do with you," came the now muffled voice. The batten of wood was knocked firmly back in place and the footsteps receded.

Chapter 6

Dougal had pitched forward, tripped on something and fallen to his hands and knees. There was no window and the darkness was complete. He groped in his pocket and pulled out his cigarette lighter. It flared into life and showed him that he was in a small boiler room. An ancient, rusty coal-fired boiler took up most of the space. On the floor was a small heap of coal, a few sticks of kindling and several heavier wooden planks of varying length. On a small shelf above the boiler was an inch-long stub of candle. Dougal lit this and slipped his lighter back into his pocket. Picking up the candle, he examined the door. It was old, but still a formidable barrier. It had a stout lock and he remembered the batten was also wedged against it outside. He wondered about using the wood at his feet as a battering-ram, but immediately gave up the idea. These planks were neither thick enough nor heavy enough.

He sat down with his back against the door and tried to think. Luck had been with him on the island and he had been fortunate to get clear of the three there. Dougal did not like to imagine what would happen when they reached the mainland. He glanced at his watch. Allowing an hour each way for the boat trip, plus a further hour if the smugglers were to salvage what they could of the drugs, he had a total of perhaps three hours, say, until 5am. He had been singularly unlucky in his choice of house from which to seek help. He knew perfectly well that the Church of Scotland, responding to the steady decline in the rural population since the first World War, had been amalgamating congregations and selling off redundant manses. However, he could hardly blame himself for not considering the possibility of this particular house being the drug-runners' base. Luck seemed to have turned against him.

As he sat there, his eyes became more accustomed to the gloom and he suddenly noticed a very rusty scissor-type car jack. Instantly, he was on his feet. With such a tool, he could bring a couple of tons pressure to bear on the door. He set about making up a framework of wood from the planks to fill the space between the boiler and the door, inserting the jack in so that its pressure would be applied, not on the lock and the batten outside, but on the hinges. As the framework was laid out on the floor, almost all the force would be on the lower of the two hinges. If that was not enough to let him out, he would have to try to devise a way of making the framework and jack apply pressure on the top hinge. There was no operating bar for the jack, but an old poker from the boiler did the job.

His first attempt ended in failure when the framework was suddenly forced upwards by the pressure and bits of wood exploded around him. Learning from this he constructed a different pattern. The hinge held and, as Dougal exerted all the force he could, the poker started to bend. Then suddenly, with a loud squeal, the screws holding the hinge pulled out of the door post and the bottom of the door jerked outwards. The noise seemed to shatter the peace of the night and Dougal devoutly hoped his assumption was correct that the man with the gun was now halfway to the island. He waited, listening for any sound. After a couple of minutes, he repositioned the frame and the jack so as to apply pressure about halfway up the door. Now operating the jack was much easier and the bottom of the door moved outwards, putting a twisting force on the top hinge The hinge held, but it bent

43

sufficiently to allow a gap of eighteen inches or so at the foot. Grateful that he was slim-built, Dougal wriggled through and was soon standing outside in the moonlight.

Now he had to decide what to do next. Instinctively he wanted to run, to put as many miles as possible between these men and himself. That's what they would expect him to do and they would try to hunt him down. There was no way they could allow him to live. He was sure of that. One course of action was to run to the village and knock up the inhabitants of the first house he came to. There were two good reasons for not doing so. The most important was that he could not hope then to preserve his anonymity. Then there was the probability that the village was inhabited by a few elderly souls who would be no match for men with guns. If he was going to phone the police, he might as well do it from the old manse itself and not involve anyone else.

Carefully, he went round, first the side, then the front of the house. It was in total darkness. He tried both doors, but they were locked. Then he noticed the kitchen window was open. He slid up the sash, and stepped into the darkened room. Drawing the blind behind him, Dougal groped his way to the door and switched on the light. At the sink, he found a pair of yellow rubber gloves. He slipped them on and, using a dish towel, wiped everything he thought he might have left finger prints on. He glanced at his watch. He still had at least an hour. The cupboard from which his captor had taken the gun might be worth checking. It was! It harboured a small arsenal. The shot-gun was gone, but he found a rifle, three revolvers and a wicked-looking machine pistol. The rifle was a fairly old service 303. The revolvers, too, looked ex-army, old, but clean and obviously serviceable. He selected two of the revolvers. They were not loaded but there was a box with fifty or more rounds in it. He loaded the guns and pushed them into his belt, wild-west fashion. Suddenly he felt a whole lot more confident.

Then he took the remaining guns, unloaded them and carried them through into the hallway. There was a cupboard under the stairs. He opened it and found it to be, like most such cupboards, full of domestic junk. Pulling this aside, he poked the guns in as far as he could. He hid the ammunition behind some books on a book-shelf in the front room. From there, Dougal went upstairs.

Picking at random one of the six doors leading off the landing, Dougal found himself in a big bedroom with a large bay window looking out over the sea. Keeping well in the shadows, he looked out. It was still very dark and, but for the full moon, he would have seen little. In the distance, he thought he could see the shape of the island. He glanced anxiously at his watch. There was still plenty of time but he felt the need to hurry. He opened a wardrobe. In it were a variety of clothes. The only thing he felt the need of was an anorak and he found one which, though a little tight round the chest and a little short in the arms, would do.

On the floor were a number of shoes. Here, however, his luck was out. The owner was at least one, if not two sizes smaller than he. No matter, his own trainers would do, although he would have preferred boots if he were to do any serious walking. Beside the shoes was a small rucksack. Thinking it would be useful, he pulled it out and opened it. Inside were several bundles of well-used five-pound notes. For a moment, Dougal wrestled with his conscience. He was not a thief. On the other hand, this gang had robbed him of his boat and very nearly taken his life as well. If he took the cash, it would barely cover his financial losses, let alone compensate him for the trauma of the past few hours.

Taking the coat and the rucksack, he pulled a heavy blanket off the bed, thrust it into the rucksack on top of the money and hurried back to the kitchen. The refrigerator was well-stocked and he transferred most of its contents along with other food into the now bulging rucksack. He would have liked to make a pot of tea, but thought that would be really pushing his luck. He slung the rucksack over his shoulder, left the kitchen by the back door and climbed up the steep back garden. At the top, a four foot dry stone wall separated garden from graveyard. He climbed over and looked back. From where he stood, he had a commanding view of the side and the rear of the house. There was a vegetable plot with a small tool-shed at the side of the house, more or less opposite the kitchen door. At the rear of the house, the steep slope was covered with unkempt grass.

Dougal laid down the rucksack on a flat gravestone. The church was between him and the road. The graveyard sloped gently up beside and behind both church and manse. Tomb-stones of varying age, size and shape stood at all sorts of angles to the vertical. The perimeter was lined with ancient and mis-shapen yews. Dougal recrossed the wall and went back to the boiler-house. Two judicious kicks and the door looked superficially secure. He then re-entered the kitchen and went upstairs. The first rays of dawn were twinkling across the bay. He peered into the gloom trying to see the boat crossing from the island to the shore. There was no sign of it. Time must be running out, he thought. Downstairs, he found a phone. He dialled 999. To the "Which service do you require?" he replied firmly, "Police."

In seconds he was through. Trying to speak with the maximum authority, Dougal said crisply, "Inspector Hewitt of Special Branch here. There's been a shooting. Drug-related incident. Get an ambulance and an armed response unit here as fast as possible. The number here is Kinloch Esk 482670. You can trace the address."

He pulled out one of the revolvers and fired a shot into an old settee. "More action! I'll have to go." And he put down the phone.

As he did so, his eye fell on a picture post-card of a country scene with a windmill beside a canal. He picked it up and read, "Having a lovely holiday. Am planning to visit the island on the 27th, weather permitting. See you soon. Love, Auntie Edith." It was addressed to 'Malcolm Scott, The Old Manse, Kinloch Esk.' It was post-marked 'Amsterdam'. It did not take a genius to work out that this was how the Scottish end of the drug smuggling operation were notified of an in-coming cargo. Under the card was an envelope containing a letter. Dougal felt he was already pushing his luck by lingering so long. He thrust the envelope into his pocket and returned to the kitchen. He switched out the light, drew back the curtains and was about to exit by the way he had entered when he heard the front door open.

Hurriedly, Dougal climbed through the window. He had barely closed it behind him when he heard footsteps coming round the side of the house. He had no time to reach the graveyard. All he could do in the seconds available was to squeeze himself behind a small ornamental bush. Three men came round the corner of the house. He realised he had been wrong in thinking that all four would enter by the front door. The three went over to the tool-shed. Two were younger men, the third being Dougal's host and captor. He was sure he would have recognised the man anyway, but the fact that he still held the shot-gun seemed to prove the point. From the shed, they took two spades and a pick-axe. Dougal felt the anger build up inside him. This was the execution and burial party. Where, he wondered, would they have buried him. In the graveyard? In silent fury, he watched as they approached. They would pass too close to his poor hiding place. He looked over his shoulder. Ten feet or so behind him was the stump of a substantial tree. It might just hide him.

As silently as he could, he slithered backwards. Just as he

reached the cover it provided, there was a shout. He had been spotted. The shot-gun roared and a hail of pellets smacked into the stump. Nearly unable to believe he had not been hit, Dougal peered round just in time to see the man with gun rushing towards him. Almost instictively, Dougal drew out a revolver and loosed off a round. There was a scream and the man fell, clutching his shoulder. Another of the gang had pulled out a gun. Dougal aimed and fired, the bullet smashing into the fellow's elbow. Meanwhile the third

man made a dive for the fallen shot-gun. He reached it and was bringing it up to his shoulder when Dougal fired again. This shot was not well aimed and hit the man in the thigh.

"Time I was off," Dougal muttered. He wiped the revolver clean, tossed it down towards the back door of the house and dashed up the garden. As he reached the wall, the back door opened and the fourth man emerged. The man took in the scene at a glance, grabbed the revolver that lay at his feet, and fired several times wildly in Dougal's direction. This time, much more deliberately, Dougal drew the second gun, he held it in both hands and, knees bent and taking careful aim, he fired one round, knocking the gun from the others's hand. He dropped the gun, then vaulted the wall and flitted noiselessly through the graveyard. Behind him came the rattle of pistol fire. Clearly, he had failed to incapacitate the fellow. Bullets whistled through the trees over his head. Something Winston Churchill had written about 'the exhilaration that comes when someone unsuccessfully shoots at you' flashed unaccountably through his mind.

Pausing only to scoop up the rucksack, he jogged rapidly up the hill. There was now no risk of pursuit by the drug-runners. The police were now the ones to evade. How many offences had he committed? Breaking and entering, theft, impersonating a police officer, illegal use of fire-arms, grievous bodily harm. The total was impressive. The need for anonymity was more compelling than ever. None of this would look good on a CV.

He followed the line of a burn up the hill, taking advantage of the cover provided by the scrub growing along its course. Only when he reached the edge of a thick spruce plantation did he pause for breath. He peeled off the rubber gloves and thrust them in his pocket. At the buildings below, there was no movement. Several houses in the village had lights on. Far away to the south down the road, he glimpsed blue flashing lights. Finding a fire-break he plunged into the plantation and worked his way up the hill.

Dougal tried to put himself in the shoes of the first senior officer on the scene. Four wounded men, with the weapons that did the damage either on them or where they might have thrown them. A clear case of thieves falling out? Dougal's knowledge of forensics was sketchy, but he was pretty sure that the experts could establish which men had fired which guns. The guns were there, as were also the drugs. The four men's involvement in criminal activity was easy to establish. However, working out the sequence of events would not be so simple.

Usually when someone is the victim of a shooting, provided they are not dead, the police would expect some help from them. What would these four say? "We were just taking this guy out to murder him and he cruelly went and shot us first?" That was hardly likely. Some story about a rival gang shooting them up and planting the drugs on them would be more like it, but such a tale would not be all that convincing. Then the police would also be asking who made the 999 call? The fact the injuries were reported fully half an hour before they were inflicted was a mystery in itself. If, by any chance, Special Branch did have an Inspector Hewitt, Dougal devoutly hoped the poor fellow had a good alibi!

All this was tumbling through his mind when he reached the top of the wood. Back down the fire-break, he could see a very narrow strip of sea. Ahead, the hill rose steeply for several hundred more feet. Climbing up that would leave him completely exposed to the view of anyone down near the foreshore. He would have to go left or right. Left, northwards into a trackless wilderness and taking him farther from Oban and his car, or south to civilisation? So southwards was the better option. But what would pursuers expect? Southwards, of course! So Dougal turned left and northwards. He trotted along the hillside, following the line of the dense pine trees for a couple of miles. There, the plantation ended at the edge of a deep gully with a raging stream roaring through it. Beyond was open country.

Very carefully, Dougal made his way down the steep side of the gully. Then he worked his way up hill, tracing the course of the torrent to the gentler slopes above. Once more, he found himself faced with an exposed tract of hill-country. The river was fordable now and, on the far side, was a line of cliffs with steep scree-slopes beneath them. He crossed over and scrambled along the foot of the scree. At various times over the centuries, vast chunks of rock had detached themselves from the cliffs and come crashing down, most shattering on impact to form the rocky scree-slope, some few remaining intact and lying where they fell, the size of small houses.

Dougal skirted round several of these enormous boulders until he found what he was looking for. One such rock had fallen across another and, beneath was a cavity, rugged but dry, that would adequately accommodate a man. He gathered a few armfuls of dry bracken and strewed them on the floor to take up some of the irregularities. He pulled the blanket he had taken from the old manse from the rucksack. He would not need it for warmth, but it would be comfortable to lie on. Then he pushed several smaller rocks into position to give greater concealment. Once satisfied with his work, he ate, drank, then settled down. There was just a chance the police might think someone involved with the shooting had taken to the hills. If they did, they might use a helicopter and they might, just, use thermal imaging equipment. Below a twenty foot slab of rock, they would not detect him. His only real fear was if they used tracker dogs. However, it would take some time to bring in dogs, so he felt reasonably safe.

Although he was tired, sleep did not come readily. He thought about the men he had cold-bloodedly shot. Dougal was totally unrepentant. They all ought to survive, but even if they did not, were they not out to kill him? A court of law might or might not see it as self-defence, but when four armed men are out to murder you, the Queensbury rules do not apply. Nor do any silly public school ideas about fair play. The only rule is the rule of the jungle. The wise man makes a pre-emptive strike. A line of poetry not found in Blackgorge High text-books came to mind.

"Twice armed is he whose cause is just,

But thrice armed he who gets his blow in fust!"

If he had any doubts, it was to the morality of leaving these men alive. The cargo they had brought ashore would almost certainly have led to at least one drug-related death if it had been allowed to reach the streets. These callous bandits would not care, so long as there was money in it for them. He thought of some of the kids from Blackgorge High. Young Alistair, for instance. His parents were leading figures in the drug scene even before he was born. They had paid a terrible price for sharing needles. AIDS and a slow and miserable death. Alistair seemed to have escaped the virus, but he was a lonely lad with a haunted look. The social services did what they could, but the loss of both parents had obviously hit the poor kid badly. Then there was Eleanor. Her mother had been notoriously selling herself for years to get her next fix and, if staff room rumour was to be believed, was now selling young Eleanor's immature little body as well. Perhaps a bullet cleanly through each skull would have been better. Certainly, it would have made Scotland a cleaner, better place. Dougal drifted off to sleep.

Chapter 7

Dougal slept like a log. Early in the afternoon, he was awakened by the unmistakable sound of a helicopter. The noise rose and fell. Obviously the machine was systematically sweeping to and fro overhead. He resisted the temptation to look out. He knew how the slightest movement on the ground could attract the eye of an alert observer in the skies. Besides, they might be using thermal imaging to detect someone hiding in the woods. Shortly after there came a throbbing heavier sound high above him which Dougal immediately recognised as being a Chinook twin-rotor helicopter. That could only mean they were flying in re-inforcements, possibly army. That, in turn, meant a land search. Despite a panicky desire to get out and run, Dougal decided to sit tight. Unless they used dogs, he would be all right. He only wished he had got rid of the rubber gloves. However, his presence cowering under a rock would be difficult to explain in itself, so perhaps it did not matter.

During a lull, when there was no sound of helicopters, Dougal cautiously looked out. There was nothing to be seen. He eased himself through the gap and out into the open. His vision was very limited because of the rock towering behind him and others of similar size to each side and below. He looked at his hiding place. What he saw, reassured him. No one who did not start excavating would so much as guess the presence of anything   bigger than a rabbit burrow. He found a rock about two foot long and a foot in diameter. He placed it by the hole before entering, feet first. Before finally drawing in his shoulders, he levered the rock and poised it so it would fall over the entrance. When he was totally inside, he rolled the rock over the gap. He could still see out of various chinks and crannies and the air would still circulate. From the outside, there would be no detecting the cavity, unless the police used dogs.

The helicopters came and went. Dougal knew that, if they had enough man-power, the choppers would be used to ferry men up and out to the perimeter of the search area. The soldiers would then start to close in on the centre of the search area, thereby forcing any fugitive into a trap, rather than driving him farther and farther away. In the early evening, he was aroused by the scuffling sound of stones trickling down the scree-slope. Someone was approaching from above. Then he heard muffled voices. He did not hear what his ears were straining for: the commands of dog-handlers. The voices grew louder. He could hear heavy footsteps. Someone was making heavy weather of keeping his footing on the shifting scree. Then, peering through a slit, he saw a large pair of army boots. He scarcely dared breathe. The boots stopped a few feet away. Then there was the sound of more footsteps. He saw another pair of boots. Then the owners of the boots sat down. There were a few muffled sounds Dougal could not identify. Then he smelt the unmistakable smell of tobacco. The squaddies had stopped for a fly smoke!

Fragments of their conversation drifted in. "I think the gang fell out among themselves. I don't believe there ever was a rival gang."

"I hope you're right. If we did stumble on them, the first thing you'd know about it would be that you'd a bullet in your guts. If they were there, I'm dashed sure they would have come and gone by car. That type are out of their depth in open country. I know the bobbies said they had set up road blocks and that no one could have got past them, but, with a decent 4 by 4, a Land Rover or the like, there must be a hundred hill-tracks they could have taken out of here."

"I don't know why we're searching so far north. If these are Glasgow gangsters, they'll have gone south. Like you say, they know the cities but wouldn't survive in the wilds."

"Better get going before we're missed, I suppose."

The two stood up. All Dougal could see were their boots and these soon disappeared. After that there was silence, broken only by the distant hiss of the stream in the gully and the occasional exuberant song of a lark. Dougal opened up the entry to his hiding place late in the evening. Across the water was the kind of heart-stopping sunset that this part of Scotland affords, when it is not raining, of course. It would be a fine night, a mixed blessing so far as Dougal was concerned. The sun dipped below the horizon. The wind fell away to nothing and a deep silence settled over the land.

Dougal packed his few possessions, consulted his compass and set off northwards along the foot of the scree-slope. He went very slowly, making no noise and stopping frequently to listen. He reached the end of the line of cliffs and of the scree. The ground rose steeply to the east. Picking a gully with a small burn in it he crept slowly upwards. Where the ground started to level out at the top was a dry stone wall running parallel with the shore and the road far below. This he approached with great caution. He stopped, lay still and listened. Then he advanced twenty yards, stopped and listened. This caution paid off. He was only yards from the wall when he heard a rustling sound ahead of him. It might be a sheep. It might be a pheasant. It might be a sentry. He waited, motionless. The sound came again. This time he heard a muffled voice. Someone was just the far side of the wall.

Very slowly and very quietly, Dougal crawled back down the hill. When he was a hundred yards from the wall, he changed direction and, in the same patient, painfully slow way, moved along in a parallel direction to it. If there were sentries bounding the east, somewhere there would be sentries bounding the north. However, they must be thin on the ground. There may have been a fair number of troops drafted in, but the perimeter they were trying to guard was so large that the gap between each must be hundreds of yards.

Once again Dougal eased his way up to the wall. This time he could hear nothing. He lay for several minutes at the foot of it. Then, still hearing nothing, he slid gently up, careful not to dislodge a stone but also careful to keep his body so close to the wall that his shape would merge into it. Once more glad of the camouflage his dark beard provided, he looked over the wall, right and left. At first he heard and saw nothing. Then, to the left, he saw a shadow detach itself from the wall nearly quarter of a mile away. He looked right. Nearer this time, a mere hundred yards away, another shadowy figure moved.

Dougal froze. It was soon apparent that he had not been spotted. For long minutes he remained motionless. Then the nearer figure started to move. For several seconds, Dougal could not determine whether the man was coming or going. At last, to his relief, he realised that the sentry was moving away from him, presumably with his back to him, although all he could see was the man's upright form. It could be his back or his front, it was impossible to tell. Nor could Dougal predict when the sentry would turn. When the gap between them had doubled, Dougal slipped off his rucksack and lowered it over the wall. Then he followed it, stretching his body along the top and lowering himself slowly and silently to the ground. With the same caution, he eased himself away from the wall and off into the long grass beyond. It took an hour to cover a quarter of a mile. After that, the pace improved. By dawn, he was three miles into the hills. He would have to assume there would be helicopter sweeps the next morning. The hillside was bleak and barren. The only hope of concealment lay in the peat hags.

Dougal pulled out the blanket purloined from the manse. It was a mid-green in colour. He laid it out on the peat in a hollow and carefully rubbed the dark brown peat into it. When he was finished, it was nearly invisible against the peat. In one wet peat bog, he rolled up his shirt sleeve, took out the yellow rubber gloves and thrust them an arms-length into the mire. He trekked on for another mile. There, on the watershed, were deep peat-hags. Where one of these had undercut the ground above, he lay down and draped his home-made camouflage blanket over him. He could do no more and so he settled down to what was to be a fitful, dream-haunted sleep.

It was the helicopters that woke him. Several times they passed over, but not sufficiently close to worry him. The long day passed slowly. As darkness descended, he rose stiffly. There was so little chance of a second line of sentries that he decided to put in as many miles as possible before daybreak. Apart from anything else, his food supplies were running low. Thirst was no problem. Every burn provided profuse supplies of wholesome water. By the time the sun rose ahead of him, he had been marching for five hours, covering three or four miles every hour. He climbed a ridge. Not wanting to be starkly visible on the skyline, he crawled the last few yards. As he lay on his stomach, looking down a long glen to a road some five miles below, a road with a few buildings on it, a wave of relief swept over him. In one of those strange flashbacks, he was suddenly lying on his stomach in a Falkland bog, gazing down in disbelief as his binoculars picked out the white flag fluttering over Port Stanley. The same wave of emotion swept over him now. He would hitch-hike south and be in Oban by evening.

Arriving at the road at break of day would attract attention.

Apart from which, he needed some rest. Skirting round an outcrop of rock, he marched off down the glen. In a deep gully on his left, a lively burn cascaded down in a series of water-falls. Under the shelter of an overhang, he lay down, pulled over his blanket and slept. He woke about noon. The sun was high in the sky and he was almost too hot. He realised he had been in his clothes, night and day for far too long. The last time they had been washed was in seawater. Small wonder he was itching! Apart from that, he must stink, hardly the ideal state for a hitch-hiker. There was no sign of life on the hills, so he stripped off and slid into a deep, inviting pool. It was marvellous! He grabbed his clothes and washed them thoroughly in the stream. After wringing them as best he could, he spread them out to dry on the warm rocks. Suddenly Dougal realised that he was feeling more alive than he had for months. The excitement of the last few days had been exhilarating. He felt half happy, half ashamed.

He lay down and sunbathed, waiting for his clothes to dry. He dozed. The doze was broken by the throb of a helicopter. It was too late to hide, besides his clothes were fluttering like so many flags. He slipped his naked body into the water. The helicopter made a low pass over him, swooped and came back even lower. The pilot grinned at him out of the cockpit and waved. Dougal waved back and smiled. The helicopter crew doubtless could not visualise desperate gun-men skinny-dipping in highland burns. After another sweep and the chopper sped off westwards.

Chapter 8

Dougal dressed and walked the remaining few miles to the road. With his rucksack on his back, he looked the genuine article and it was not long before he was speeding past Loch Maree and heading for Inverness in a Ford Mondeo. Again, he was glad of his beard. Had he been in the habit of shaving, four day's growth would have taken some explaining. The Mondeo was driven by the north Scotland representative of an agricultural chemicals supplier who chatted away happily, glad of the company. He dropped Dougal off at the turning for Fort William at the northern outskirts of Inverness late in the afternoon. Dougal was starving so he found a fish and chip shop and ate a hearty meal. Suddenly he remembered old Angus. He had better phone him before the old chap called out the coast-guard.

Angus answered promptly, "Dougal, is that you? My! Man, am I glad to hear your voice. When thon storm blew up out of nowhere, man, I was fair worried about you. Then when you didn't call! Well! I didn't know whether to call out the coastguard or what. Where are you now, laddie?"

"Angus, I'm heart sorry not to have called before, but this is the first time I've been near a call box. I've a long tale to tell. Too long for a phone call. I've lost 'Monica'. She's at the bottom of the Minch."

"Well, at least she's not taken you with her, thank the Lord! Where are you now?"

"Inverness. I doubt if I can get a bus that will get me down there tonight so I'll stay in Inverness until morning. I'll tell you the rest when I see you."

"Do you have enough money? I assume all your gear went down with the boat."

Dougal thought quickly. He had wads of used fivers in the rucksack but there was no way he wanted to explain that to Angus. The old fellow would be appalled!

"Enough for the fare," he replied. "It's a fine night and I'm getting used to sleeping under the stars!"

"Look, if you're in Inverness, that's fine. My nephew will give you a hand. Let me call him. What's the number of your phone box there?" Suddenly Dougal felt too weary to turn down any offer of help. He gave Angus the number and leant on the outside of the phone box to await the return call.

A few minutes later the phone rang. "I've spoken to my nephew. He's expecting you. You'll find him easy enough. He lives round the back of Tomnahurich. Here's the address."

Gratefully, Dougal noted it down. He ate some bread and walked slowly towards the wooded hill of Tomnahurich, wondering what sanitised version of events he should tell both Angus and his nephew. Angus's nephew was a middle-aged accountant, a small man who looked as if he was permanently stooped, perhaps through bending over books all day. His welcome was heart-warmingly cheerful.

"Hello, there. I'm Stuart Morris. My uncle tells me you've fallen on hard times! It's not often we get ship-wrecked mariners washed up on our door-step! Come away in and meet the wife."

Mrs Morris was even smaller than her husband, a lively looking woman with a merry twinkle in her eye. "We were about to eat. It's chicken, so there's more than enough for the three of us. I hope you've not eaten? Good, come away in. Stuart, how about drinks? I'm sure Mr Henderson would like a sherry or something. You see to it while I strain the vegetables"

Feeling a little out of place in the meticulously tidy home, Dougal gratefully accepted the proffered sherry. Despite the fish and chips he had eaten earlier, he needed no appetiser. The smell from the kitchen had his mouth watering. Soon the three were sitting down to a substantial meal. During dinner, Dougal gave a dramatic account of the storm. He made no reference to being rammed, to drug smugglers or his flight over the hills. He explained his delay in contacting Angus by telling of being wrecked on an unnamed island, [nearly true], being stranded for three days, [not true], and of getting back to the mainland by fishing boat, [true, but hardly the truth, the whole truth and nothing but the truth]. The couple listened enthralled. Dougal could tell a good story and they were spell-bound.

"I didn't see any of this in the papers," said Mrs Morris. "I would have thought they would have leapt at a story like that."

Dougal had anticipated this. "Well, to tell the truth, I've tried to suppress it. Only the chaps who own the fishing boat know. My boat wasn't insured. Well, wasn't insurable, if the truth were told. I don't want any conservationists demanding that she be salvaged so as not to pollute the Atlantic. You know what they're like! With no insurance, I'd have to pay a fortune for finding her and then raising her. She's only fit for scrap anyway."

"I understand," said Morris. "There is such a thing as going too far when it comes to conservation. Good economic sense should prevail in cases like this. All the conservation lobby do with some of their wilder demands is to alienate the vast majority of sensible people and that damages their own cause. Just keep quiet and I'm sure you'll be all right. It does sound as if you've had a narrow escape, though."

"You can say that again," said Dougal with deep feeling.

"Probably a closer call than you can imagine! I know I'm lucky to be alive. Perhaps next time I'll take heed to what your uncle says!"

The evening passed pleasantly and Dougal was glad to get to bed at an early hour. He could hardly remember when he last slept in a bed and was soon sound asleep. In the morning, after a hearty breakfast, his host gave him a lift to the bus station. He insisted on lending Dougal £50 which Dougal accepted, that being easier than explaining his ample supply of five pound notes. Three hours later, Dougal was telling his equivocal version of events to Angus. When he had finished, the old man sat looking at him for several minutes without saying a word. Then he spoke.

"Aye, well. That story will do fine for the likes of my nephew, but I think you should now be telling me the truth."

Dougal squirmed. The old man was a walking lie-detector. For some minutes neither said a word. Then Dougal told the story from the beginning, leaving out nothing except the five-pound notes, embellishing nothing, excusing nothing. There was another long silence. At last, the old man answered.

"Well, you've had quite a bit of excitement. I can see why you don't want this to get out. I've no idea whether the police would charge you for shooting those four. I've a feeling they would say you shouldn't have, but I'm not going to sit in judgement. I don't know what I would have done if it had been me. I'd like to think I would have been as brave, but I'm not sure. Anyway, I don't think we need tell anyone. Mind you, I'm not saying I'll lie for you if I'm asked a direct question by someone in authority, but I cannot see that happening. You go away back home and don't worry about a thing. By the by, will you be buying another boat?"

"Not just now. Perhaps next year. I've had enough excitement for one summer. Perhaps I've used up my ration of luck for this year! No. I'll let you know, but it would be next spring at the earliest"

"I just wondered. Old George McGregor's awful bad with rheumatics. He's talking about selling his yacht. Think about it and let me know. I'll have a word with him for you if you like. He'd want it to go to a good home."

Thanking the old man profusely for all his help, Dougal took his leave. Fortunately, his car key had been in the pocket of his jeans and had survived all the adventures of recent days. Soon Dougal was speeding homeward.

Chapter 9

Some eight weeks before Dougal had weighed anchor and set sail for Tobermory, the bankruptcy sale at a medium-sized printers had taken place in North London. The long established Nimrod Press had gone under and the receivers had left it to one of the specialist printers' auctioneers to sell the plant and machinery. As is usual on these not infrequent occasions, a mixed bag of printers, printing machinery dealers and others had assembled, vulture-like, to see what they could pick up at a knock-down price.

Nimrod Press, like almost every printing business in the land, had suffered badly in the recessions of the 1990's. Much of their plant was old, though doubtless well-maintained and still serviceable. The typesetting equipment was largely obsolete, as was most of the pre-press machinery such as cameras, plate-makers, printing-down frames etc. That did not mean it was very old. Machinery over three years old was already obsolete due to the coming of the computer-age. The staggeringly fast development of computerised-typesetting and other equipment had brought about a revolution. The one big perpetual problem for any such printer in such a capital-intensive industry was how to keep reasonably up to date.

Nimrod Press had tried, but conspicuously had failed. The printing machinery was an interesting mixture of ancient and modern. There were one or two presses which would look more at home in a museum than in a modern printing factory. Several of the others dated from the sixties and seventies. The only really modern presses were a couple of Heidelberg GTOs from the early nineties. Ask any printer which is the best litho press and, ten to one, he will say 'Heidelberg'. The GTOs were the second smallest press in the wide range manufactured in the city whose name they bear. Unlike the typesetting and pre-press equipment, the development of the litho press had not been so dramatic as to leave seven or eight year old machines hopelessly outclassed. On the contrary, they were highly efficient and could still compete favourably with their most up-to-date counterparts.

Nimrod Press had prospered in the boom years of the eighties. When recession loomed, the directors had taken the bold decision to re-equip with the state-of-the-art GTOs. They had borrowed heavily and bought two of these machines. These were high-speed four-colour machines capable of turning out top-quality coloured illustrations at very low cost. The decision to buy had been courageous and, if the boom had only continued, the gamble would have paid off. But business took a nose-dive. All over the country, there were competing printers, each with hungry presses, all chasing whatever work could be had. There was simply not enough work to go round. Nimrod could not earn enough to keep up their payments to the finance house and so the twin presses were now for sale to the highest bidder.

The sale opened, as is usual on such occasions, with the sale of the low-value and least attractive items. It was therefore well on in the day when the auctioneer announced, "Now we come to Lot 143, the Heidelberg GTO 52 with alcohol damping. This machine is in superb order, having been bought new in 1990 by Nimrod Press and used only on single shift operations. It has recorded a mere 36 million impressions and, as all you ladies and gentlemen know, that is nothing to any Heidelberg! Now, what shall we say for this machine. £160,000? £150,000? £140,000?

£130,000? Well, someone start me. £85,000! Thank you, sir. £85,000 I'm bid. £90,000 on my left. £95,000. At £95,000 now. The bids with you, sir, at the front. £100,000. £105,000. £105,000 at the back. No, sir! The bid's against you. £105,000, thank you, madam. At £105,000. £105,000. Any advance on £105,000. Going, then at £105,000. Ah! £110,000. New bidder at £110,000. Against you, madam. £110,000 Any more? Well then, for the first time. £110,000. For the second time £110,000. Are you all over and out at £110,000? Sold then at £110,000. Name, please? Rupert Smithers & Company? Thank you, sir."

A ripple of conversation ran round the building. A good machine, but dear at £110,000. That seemed to be the consensus, at least among the dealers.

"Now Lot No 144. Another Heidelberg GTO 52, again with alcohol damping. The sister machine to the previous lot. Bought new by Nimrod at the same time and having less than 33 million impressions on it. Now, who'll start me. £140,000? £130,000? Now, ladies and gentlemen. You don't need me to remind you that these machines do not come on the market very often and low-mileage presses like these are as rare as hen's teeth! £80,000? Well, where do you want to start? £70,000, thank you, madam. £70,000 I'm bid. £75,000. £80,000. £85,000. £90,000. £95,000. £100,000. At £100,000. It's the lady's bid at £100,000. At £100,000. £105, 000. At £105,000. The bid's against you madam. I'll take a £2,000 if that will help. £107,000. Thank you, madam! £109,000. £109,000. At £109,000. Are you all finished then at £109,000?" Bang! The hammer fell with a finality. "Sold! Same buyer."

With the cream of the plant sold, most of the potential buyers began to drift away. The successful bidder for the two Heidelbergs wrote out a cheque for £238,000, paying for the two presses together with a collating machine and a Polar guillotine. He telephoned his insurers and had the equipment added to his policy.

Four days later, the cheque having been cleared by the Bank, the receiver arranged for the bidder's engineer to get access to the machines. This engineer spent the whole day dismantling all four machines and preparing them for transportation. The following day, he completed the work and the first of the Heidelbergs was loaded on a lorry and removed to its new home. Two days later, the buyer phoned the receivers. His engineer was ill. Would it be all right to delay the removal of the rest for a week? There was no problem about this and the matter was left there.

During the night, a very professional thief visited the deserted premises of the late, lamented Nimrod Press. Very professionally, the burglar alarm was put out of action and the thief melted away into the night as silently as he had come. The following morning, a van and a lorry with a Hiab crane mounted on it drew up outside the printing factory. A jemmy soon had the double doors standing wide. The three remaining machines were lined up ready for loading. The occasional passer-by may have given the overall-clad workman a glance, but there was nothing suspicious about the removal of machinery from a defunct factory. A careful observer might have had his interest aroused by two facts. The engineers all wore gloves and, secondly, they worked with a rapidity unusual among British workmen.

Certainly, within an hour, all three items of plant were not only on the lorry but were secured and covered by a tarpaulin. The factory doors were closed. A daub of greasy dirt masked the jemmy marks. The engineers crowded into the back of the van. Both the lorry driver and the van driver seemed to have heavy colds. At any rate, they held handkerchiefs to their faces until they were three blocks away.

Four days later, the buyer's engineer and a clerk from the receiver met outside Nimrod's premises. They entered by the office door and so did not notice the evidence of the break-in. The clerk pulled on the main electricity switch. His jaw dropped. Where there should have been three machines, there were only a few oily marks on the concrete floor.

Chapter 10

"Do you know what a Heidelberg GTO is?" Detective Inspector Flint asked his long-time friend, Alfred Reid.

"Of course I do. Asking a printer if he knows what a Heidelberg is must be a bit like asking a policeman if he knows what a Ford Escort is! We've got a couple of GTOs and several of their bigger brothers as well. Why do you ask?"

The two friends had met at Flint's request at their usual watering hole and were enjoying a pint at the end of the day.

"Because someone has nicked one."

"What, nicked a printing press? However did he manage it? You can't just nip into a printers and shop-lift something like that. Apart from anything else, it must weigh at least a ton. In fact it would be three or four times more if it were a multi-colour press."

"It was a four-colour. It had been sold at auction. The owners were in receivership. The machine was dismantled ready for transport and when the receiver and the engineer went to pick it up, it had simply vanished. Any ideas as to who would pinch something like that?"

Reid looked gloomy. "I don't give much for your chances of finding it. There's a terrific demand world-wide for any kind of Heidelberg. It's probably printing in Arabic in a Middle East bazaar by now."

"Hardly likely," the detective replied. "We reckon it's only been gone three days, perhaps four at the most. What makes you think it will have gone abroad?"

" I remembered an article in Lithoweek. That's one of the trade magazines. It was a few years back, maybe about 1990. More or less what you've described, but this machine was a monster. I can't remember the model, but it was one of the largest machines Heidelberg make. The river police found a water-logged Thames barge at a disused wharf. It had been abandoned. In it, was this beautiful Heidelberg with the river flowing through it. Seems the thieves hadn't done their home-work. There must have been a freighter lying off the mouth of the river waiting for it. The press was just too heavy for the barge and it sunk at the quayside under the weight. The thieves scarpered, of course, and the police were left to try to find out who had not yet missed fifty tons of Heidelberg. Same story. Once the property of bankrupt printers. Sold at auction and waiting in the unused factory for the new owner to uplift it. I'd love to have seen his face when they opened the door and found only sixty foot of space where there should have been sixty foot of Heidelberg!"

"I'll check up on that. It might give us a lead. As you say, there are similarities." Flint raised his glass to his lips and sipped thoughtfully. "They also took a Polar guillotine and a Bourg collator. I know what a guillotine is, but what's a collator?"

"It's a machine for putting sets of papers in order. Suppose you have a set of forms which you want in triplicate, top copy white, middle blue and the bottom green. Even if the wording on all three is identical, the printer obviously prints the white, then the blue, then the green. He's left then with three piles of paper. He loads them into the collator. It picks up a green sheet and lays it down. Then it picks up a blue sheet and lays it on top of the green. Then it picks up a white sheet and lays it on the blue. Then it's back to the green and so on. Probably handling 10,000 sheets an hour. So all you need to do is to figure out who wants to print, cut and collate. Narrows the field down to about 95% of the printers in the country! I'm glad to have been of help! By the way, it's your round, I think."

When Flint returned from the bar he found his friend lost in thought. Eventually he looked up and said, "Whoever stole these machines must either have had a ready market or be the end-user. Heidelbergs are superb machines, but sooner or later it'll need spare parts. When that happens, the printer has no real option but to go to the makers, Heidelberg themselves. Now all these machines are being continuously up-dated, so Heidelberg always ask for the machine number if you order anything. With typical German efficiency, they then check every modification that may have been done to your particular press and make sure you get the right bit. This means that they must know where virtually every one of their machines is. This will be a real problem if your friend needs a part. He obviously can't quote the right number. Heidelberg will learn soon enough the machine's been stolen. He daren't give a fictitious number because Heidelberg will know where the machine with that number is. I can only assume that the thief or his customer already has a machine of similar age and of the same specification so he can, if necessary, quote its number. There! That's probably reduced your number of suspect printers to something more manageable! Mind you, I still think you should watch the ports."

"It may be long enough before the thing needs spares. Any thoughts about the Polar or the Bourg collator?"

"Polar is another Heidelberg product. First-class machines. The same thing would apply to spares for it, but these things seldom go wrong. The blades need regular sharpening, of course. Only a very large printing company would sharpen its own. Every decent size city has an engineering company sharpening blades. You've no real chance of getting a lead that way. Blades are anonymous things. The engineers have no way of telling what machine a particular blade is from. It could be from any one of dozens of guillotines of the same size. The collator won't help much either. They do break down, but any competent engineer can mend them, without reference to the manufacturers. No. If you are going to try and trace the whereabouts of the stolen stuff by checking on spares, it's the Heidelberg or nothing. It might be worth asking Heidelberg for a list of GTO customers. It will be yards long, but you might spot someone dodgy."

"The guy who bought it at the auction is nearly in that category. No previous convictions, but he's sailed fairly close to the wind on one or two of his business ventures. Keeps some pretty dodgy company, too. Again, more what we used to call spivs rather than outright crooks. You know, the kind who would not pass the 'would you buy a second-hand car from this man?' test!"

Flint paused and then added thoughtfully, "Interesting, when you come to think about it. He bought an identical press in the same sale. He paid up and his cheque cleared. Part of the money was his own and part a bank loan. Nothing unusual there. All the machines were insured as soon as he bought them, but that's just the act of any prudent businessman. No doubt the insurers will pay up. They can hardly do otherwise."

"Slightly unusual, buying two identical machines at the same time. They're high-output presses. Did he say where the work to keep them busy is coming from? I certainly wouldn't know how to accelerate my own business sufficiently rapidly to soak up the surplus capacity of a couple of four-colour GTOs. That kind of growth usually comes gradually."

"He said he's going heavily into full-colour work. He's bought out a reprographic studio which had become over-stretched financially because it had been buying state-of-the-art plate-making equipment. Now he reckons he's got a set up that will give him a real competitive edge."

"Sounds plausible. He can hardly have the two presses and no one notice! Could he have a friend who needs a press?"

"I don't see how any printer in the country could suddenly bring in a machine like that without his staff wondering where it came from," replied Flint. "In due course, the whole business is bound to be reported widely in the trade press. Possibly your export theory is the most likely. I know it goes on a lot with contractors' plant. Sometimes the export paper-work for a bulldozer is completed right down to chassis and engine numbers before the thing's even stolen. Then it disappears one Friday night and is building roads in Spain by the time it's missed on Monday morning! This Heidelberg is a bit different, though. The thieves couldn't have foreseen that the engineer who was legitimately moving it would take ill and that the machine would be sitting there ready for uplifting. The whole business is a bit puzzling. Anyway. That's enough shop-talk for one evening. Are you golfing this week-end?"

And, with that, the conversation moved on to more conventional topics.

Chapter 11

Inspector Flint was making no progress on the case of the stolen printing machinery. When he visited the company that had purchased the machine at the auction, whilst he felt there was something cagey and defensive about the replies to his questions, there was not a shred of hard evidence to suggest that anything untoward was going on. He probed more deeply into the background of the company. Rupert Smithers & Company Limited had been established about a century ago. The founder, his son and, eventually, his grandson had built up a reputation for reliability and quality. They had not built up a personal fortune in the process.

Flint's enquiries into the printing trade came as something of a revelation to him. Britain's printing industry is a major employer of labour, but the vast majority of printing firms employ less than fifty of a staff. Many employ less than twenty. Most companies are run by their owners personally and these men and women often work ridiculously long hours to keep their businesses afloat. Many would earn vastly more over a working lifetime if they were in someone else's employ and put in the same effort and hours. The desire for independence would, it seems, be the spur that kept them slaving for themselves.

More than once, Flint heard the tale of the printer who came from a deprived background, worked long hours for sixty years, built up a business employing forty people and died leaving a million and a half pounds. The trade press, in its obituary column, attributed this wealth to a lifetime of determination, hard work, punishingly long hours, dedication to the needs of the customers - and to a two million pound win on the pools.

The third generation of Smithers had retired about seven years ago. There was no fourth generation to take over and the business had been sold. The new proprietor had various business interests and buying a virtually non-profit making printing company seemed a strange move. Henry Robson, Harry to his friends, was in his early forties. He had started his working life helping his uncle who had a stall in the local openair market. Harry had graduated from there, first to having his own stall, then to having a shop, then to wheeling and dealing in dubious merchandise, mostly from the Far East and mostly sold to professional car-boot traders, a growing market in the entrepreneurial Britain of the Thatcher years. It was a highly profitable business for Harry and, being mainly transacted in cash, was not too demanding so far as bookkeeping was concerned. Indeed, his standard of living was somewhat at odds with his contributions to the public purse in the form of income tax and VAT. With that kind of background, it was surprising that he had gone into the unprofitable world of printing.

Any competent accountant could have told him that the printing industry was nearly as bad as farming when it came to a decent return on capital. Harry's own explanation was that he always fancied printing. Well, that was no less logical than the motivation of most of his peers in the printing trade. It just seemed to ring a little untrue when put alongside the unquestionable truth that Harry always fancied money, easy money for preference.

On one of his visits to Rupert Smithers & Co., Flint took Alfred Reid with him, airily introducing him as 'my technical advisor'. The two spent some time looking at the other GTO. It had been reassembled since having been moved from Nimrod Press and was churning out impressively good full-colour brochures, the blank sheets of paper going in at one end and the finished job coming out the other at a speed of 7,000 sheets per hour. As Flint interviewed Harry, Alfred chatted to the operator of the GTO.

"Great machines, these," he opened with. "Had any teething problems?"

"No, not really. There were one or two adjustments to be made, as you would expect. Machines don't like being moved. It's fine now and a vast improvement on the old Falcon it replaced. I used to think the Falcon was not a bad machine, but give me one of these any day!"

"Are you the only operator?" Alfred asked. He looked round at the rest of the staff, all busy on various items of plant, but none of them actually printing.

"Yes. This machine more than copes with the work. We used to have three machine men and two single-colour and one two-colour machine. I can now turn out more than the three put together! One of the other chaps was due for retiring. The other had not been here long. He was with Watsons' Reprographics. That's the repro house the boss took over last year. The guy was brilliant at the repro side and not too bad as a machine man. He was to be running the press that was nicked. When it went, there was only work for one of us. I don't mind telling you that I was a bit worried that the boss would keep him and let me go. I argued for 'last in, first out', seeing the other chap was technically employed here for less than a year. I'm glad to say, I won."

"The other fellow wouldn't have too much trouble finding a job, though, would he?" Alfred asked. "What with him being a good all-rounder on both pre-press and machining?"

"Things are not easy, as I'm sure you know. He's gone somewhere in Scotland, but I can't remember where."

"Is Watsons' Reprographics still functioning?" Alfred

asked.

"Yes and no," was the ambiguous reply. "The place was closed down a couple of months back and all the gear moved in here. There is some really up-to-the-minute digital plate-making. I don't pretend to understand it, but the remaining Watson employee is a genius on it. I just get the plates, stick them on the machine and I don't think I've ever had a duff one from him."

Flint had finished his conversation with Harry and the two took their leave. Once in the car and on the road, Flint asked, "Well, what do you think?"

"An impressive set-up! That machine man knows his job and they're doing good work. He showed me samples of some of their recent jobs. Good stuff! I'd have been really proud to have done any of them."

"Anything strike you as dodgy?"

"No. Not really," replied Alfred thoughtfully. "If I'm any judge of character, that guy's as straight as a die. The one thing that puzzles me is why they were going to buy two GTOs. He's turning out more on that one GTO than they used to do with three men and three machines. The other minor thing is that Robson does not strike me as a man who would hesitate to sack any employee if it suited him, yet he kept the less versatile of the two machine men and fired the other. That seems strangely out of character. The other apparently went without a murmur. These days that's surprising."

"Might be worth an enquiry or two. I'll find out who the machine man is and where he's gone. Robson's insurers have accepted the claim as valid and he's expecting a cheque from them any day. It's a bit humiliating to have to admit to both the loss adjuster and Robson that we're no further forward, but, I'm afraid, we're not."

Chapter 12

The local employment office provided the information that the machine man whose job was forfeit when his machine was stolen, had signed on, but that they had lost sight of him when he had moved north. Further enquiries at national level failed to establish whether he was working or drawing unemployment money. Flint was fairly sure that the truth was that they had lost the fellow somewhere in their system, but were unwilling to admit such a possibility to the police. Apart from knowing his name, David Hawdon, they were really no further forward. It was not a very promising line of enquiry anyway, as it was highly unlikely that Hawdon could provide any information they did not already have. There the matter rested.

David Hawdon was not resting, however. Two days after the theft of the printing machine, Harry had paid him off with a generous redundancy lump sum. Hawdon then went by train to Leeds. From there, he went via Settle, to Carlisle. There, he was picked up at the station by a nondescript character in an old mini and driven to a disused warehouse. The keys of a waiting lorry were handed over and soon Hawdon was in Scotland, driving up the M74, by-passing Glasgow, Stirling and Perth, heading north up the A9 towards Inverness. He left the main road near Aviemore and drove on, the roads becoming increasingly narrow.

Eventually, he turned off the public road in through the dilapidated gates of a shooting lodge, passing a sign-post so weathered as to be almost illegible which read 'Altnariach'. The house itself, a Victorian neo-gothic monstrosity, had fallen victim to a fire many years before. He skirted round past the gaunt ruins and arrived at a stable block at the rear. Here he was faced with a high castellated wall with strong closed double doors set in it. He alighted and banged on the door. A few minutes later it was opened a few inches. A red-haired lad of about nineteen looked out through the gap. When he saw David Hawdon, he flung the door right back and set about opening the other.

"Have a good run up, David?" He asked. "The traffic on the A9 can be bad, what with all the caravans and tourists."

"Hullo, Brian. No, it was really not bad at all. The worst bit was getting to Carlisle. Why Harry thinks all the cloak-and-dagger stuff of changing trains and buses is necessary, I don't know. There's nothing to connect Harry and me with the business at Nimrod's. Anyway, I'm here now. Any chance of something to eat? Harry told me not to stop for food in case anyone remembered me at a service station. He's paranoiac and I'm starving!"

The two garaged the lorry in one of the commodious coach-houses and they went up an outside stair to what had obviously been a stable-man's quarters. At the top of the steps, David turned and looked down on the yard below. It was a hundred yards long and thirty wide. On both sides were doors to stables, coach-houses, harness rooms and so on. The buildings on the south side were two storey. Those on the north side were different. About half at the west end were stables, having hay-lofts above, each with a distinctive dormer-type door with a jib and pulley above it for bales of hay to be hoisted up. The other half, at the east end, were the old coach-houses, with ten-foot high doors and correspondingly high ceilings, an indication of the opulence and size of the horse-drawn coaches they had once housed. This part of the building was single storey, but the pitched roof was almost the same height as that above the hay-lofts.

On the south side where David stood, the upper-floor must have provided the living quarters of the ghillies, stalkers, stable-boys and all the other lesser species of Victorian rural life. They must have been little men then, he thought as he had to duck his head to get into the attic room. Inside it was cheerful enough, being small, low-ceilinged but comfortable. In a corner was a butane stove at which his red-headed companion busied himself. Soon the smell of frying filled the small room. In the corner was a carton of beer cans and David settled down with one and put his feet up.

A few minutes later, Brian dished up a plain but filling meal. "This is the best I can do at short notice," he said with a grin. "Actually, I eat quite well. There's several acres of scrub woodland around the place and I bag a pheasant or a duck every so often. There's loads of them around, what with the bird sanctuary and the marshes being so near. You wait until the week-end and I'll do a roast duck."

"How did Harry come by this place?" David asked, as the two settled down to eat.

"Quite a good set-up, don't you think?" His cook replied. "Seems some arty chap who fancied the good life away from the rat-race of the south bought the place and thought he could make a living doing ornamental iron-work. The Highlands and Islands Development Board gave him a grant, but it's too far off the beaten track to pay. The one good thing is that the Development Board paid for the installation of three-phase power."

"How long ago was that?" David asked.

"Five or six years, I think. There have been at least two other optimists since. One, I do know, was a sort of artists' commune. That fairly shocked the locals. Free love, alcohol and drugs, without a decent picture being produced. Another batch of Development Board hand-outs, I suppose. Harry got the place for a song, not that anyone knows that he's the ultimate owner. Farther down the drive, there's the remains of a walled garden. Harry's got some crack-pot who fancies himself as a potter established in the old potting sheds. The fellow lives in that gate-house you passed. When he's sober, he potters. Shouldn't wonder if Harry got a grant for him too! Anyway, his ovens are enough to prevent any nosy electricity board employee wondering at the size of our bills. The locals think I'm an artist. Harry sends photographs of Scottish scenes to Taiwan and gets back oil and water colours, all with my signature in the bottom corner. Every so often, I take a few and hawk them round the tourist traps and the galleries in Aviemore and Grantown. I only hope some art expert doesn't suddenly 'discover' me! That would be really embarrassing!"

"And how long have you been here?"

"Nine months, now. Ever since Harry got tired of being ripped off by the Thais for his soft porn. I've turned out some quite good work on his old Solna. It's only a two-colour and the register's not too hot. The rollers are clapped out and the ink-duct keys ropey. The punters don't seem to mind. As long as they get their kicks, it doesn't bother them if the cyan is weak and the magenta too strong! Harry has hinted that we're to be moving up-market, but hasn't said what. The collator came last week. What the devil does he want with a collator? It doesn't like art paper. Mis-feeds it something dreadful, so I hope he's not planning to sell packs of ten assorted girlie prints. There was also a big blocking press and a life-supply of silver blocking foil delivered last week. No explanation for that, either. What's he up to, I wonder?"

"Then wonder on, 'till truth makes all things plain'," said David who, for a criminal, albeit with no convictions yet, displayed a remarkable liking for Shakespeare.

Brian Cooper had come into the pornography business early in life. Even before he left school, he had a Saturday job with a jobbing printer who made a few pounds, Monday to Friday, when his six of a staff were there to help him. However, he made a small fortune on Saturdays when, initially single-handed and later with Brian as his keen unofficial apprentice, he knocked off the soft porn that his old school chum, Harry Robson, had such a ready market for. It had all come to an end when Brian's boss dropped dead one Saturday. With remarkable presence of mind for one so young, Brian did not phone for an ambulance. He phoned Harry. The ambulance and police did come, but only after every scrap of evidence had been spirited away. The delay making a 999 call was easily explained by Brian's statement that he had been delayed while getting lunch from the take-away for his boss. Harry was grateful and recognised talent when he saw it. Brian was well looked after and had no regrets.

Chapter 13

David Hawdon slept well. The silence of the remote shooting lodge and its stables was almost unnerving. When he awoke, he dressed and went out the door to survey his new home. He stood on the landing at the top of the steps leading down into the stable-yard below. Beyond the castellated wall on his left, the ground fell away steeply. At the foot was a wide   drainage ditch with such peaty water in it that it was impossible to hazard a guess at its depth. Beyond, there was a mixture of poor quality grassland and pools of dark brown water. Then, farther still, in the distance, was a flood-plain with a river flowing sluggishly through it. Flocks of birds spiralled over the water and the pools were dotted here and there with white which he rightly assumed to be swans. To the right, the ground rose gently at first, then more steeply to some impressively high mountains, the peaks of which were obscured in swirling cloud. The sun was fighting a losing battle with the clouds and it looked like rain. Perhaps the castellations and the Scottish scenery brought 'Macbeth' to mind. "So fair and foul a day, I have not long time seen," he muttered to himself.

After a decent breakfast, David and Brian set to work. The lorry had to be unloaded and returned to Carlisle. They soon had the tarpaulin off and, using the Hiab, the four units the Heidelberg were lowered on to steel rollers on the concrete in the yard. Fortunately, although the sky grew darker, the rain held off. By mid-day, the press was safely in one of the stables. It was soon followed by the guillotine. As they folded the tarpaulin, the first heavy spots of rain began to fall. David looked at his watch. Nearly 3pm. A full hour ahead of schedule. There was time for a break before he drove south. Brian disappeared with a shotgun. Several minutes later came the sound of distant shots. After a further interval, Brian returned, grinning all over his face, with a brace of pheasants in one hand and the shotgun in the other.

"I'll hang these for a few days and then I'll show you what kind of a cook I am!"

Later on that evening, David drove into the motorway service area at Stirling. He parked the lorry in the appropriate part for commercials and wandered over to the main building. He was still ahead of time so he ate a leisurely meal in the restaurant. At 9pm he walked out and stood looking at the rain. A familiar figure came sprinting in. It was Geordie, another of Harry's lot.

"Hi! How goes it," said David.

"Fine! Just fine! I saw your lorry and I've parked the Transit beside it. The paper's at the front. Two pallets. The washing machines are at the back. I don't suppose you're going to tell me what Harry's doing with old washing machines? No? I thought not! Ah! well. That's his business. Perhaps it's best not to know, where Harry's concerned. We'd better get going. It'll be after midnight before I'm in Carlisle. Have you got far to go?"

David gave a non-committal answer. It was, as Geordie said, better that he should not know more than he had to of Harry's business. It was nearly 1am before he garaged the Transit in one of the stables and went to bed.

The following morning, David and Brian made a late start. Over a leisurely breakfast, David filled the young chap in on Harry's latest scheme. "Fivers! We're going into the Mint business. Lots and lots of lovely fivers! Now, you're the expert! Tell me what the problems of producing fivers are."

Brian thought for a minute. "Paper," he said. "Where do you get the watermarked paper with the metal line running through it? The printing's no great problem. You'll never turn out anything that would get past an expert, but, when you think that chancers have managed to pass off colour photo-prints in badly-lit pubs, anything we do would fool your average punter. The numbering is a different matter." He pulled out a battered wallet and extracted a five pound note. "I take it you mean Bank of England fivers? Not the mickey mouse Scottish bank notes? Right! Well, it's numbered in two places, one set of numbers horizontal and one vertical. The quality of the numbering is the major difficulty. It's the same quality as the rest of the print, not your usual numbering box job, with the digits not aligning properly. I don't know much about numbering machines, but I imagine that whilst you might get something that does the horizontal batch, there would be no commercial demand for the vertical and even enquiring about such machines would attract attention."

"A good potted summary of the problems," said David. "Let's take them one by one. The paper is good quality, but not difficult to match with an unwatermarked equivalent. You can't add a watermark, but if you print the watermark design on with a mixture of thick white grease and transparent matt varnish, you get something not unlike the real thing. The metal line is, of course, impossible. Try tearing that note at the line. You see! It is an actual strip of metal running through the paper, part of it visible and part in the heart of the paper. No! We can't do that, but we can foil-block a silver line and then over-print it with opaque white, giving the impression its integral with the paper. That's where the blocking press comes in. The numbers are a headache, but we're going to print those litho."

"You mean all the notes will have the same number? That's just daft! You'll never pass more than a few hundred."

"No, it's more complicated and more cunning than that. We print the notes ten on a sheet, full colour both sides, at the same time printing the pre-fixes which, if you look at that note, you will see, consist of two letters and two numbers printed in dark green. We're printing ten on a sheet, so that gives us ten varieties already. We then run the sheet through again, printing the last two digits of the number. The horizontal are red and the vertical blue/green, so we use two units of the press. On the first note we print 10, the second 20, the third 30 and so on up to the tenth, which is 00. We run a tenth of the job and change the plates to print 11, 21, 31 and so on up to 10. Another change of plates, and we have 12, 22, 32 etc. When we've run all the paper through, we have ten piles numbered from 00 to 99. Then the collator does its job. We collate the sheets so that we have numbers 00 to 99 in each set of ten. We then start the whole process again, this time inserting the third and fourth digits. They, too are in red and blue/green, so we use two units. Collate again and then do the final set. The colour changes subtly on the second of these, so we use a third unit. Clever, don't you think?"

"That means that there are still an awful lot with the same number, though, doesn't it?" Brian asked thoughtfully.

"Yes, but a final collating exercise before we cut them down to singles will shuffle the packs so thoroughly, that the end distributors should have very few duplicates. The arithmetic is quite complicated but, if I've got it right, there should be one thousand different numbers. That's only 100 notes the same in every £100,000."

"And where do the washing machines come in?"

"Yes! That's the really cunning bit. Adds a new dimension to the term 'money-laundering'! When anyone gets a batch of brand new notes with consecutive numbers, they look at them twice. Newly printed notes suggest forgery, even when they've come straight from the bank. But give a chap a well-used grubby fiver. Does he hold it up to the light? Well, he might, but he won't be surprised if the watermark is indistinct. Used notes look more genuine than new ones. After we've guillotined ours, they go into the washing machines with a mix of slightly oily rags, damp sawdust and good old garden soil. The machines have been reprogrammed to tumble the contents gently around. There's no spin cycle. By trial and error, we've found the right mix and right length of time to convert brand new notes to well-used ones. It's a bit of a plaster, but it's vital to the success of the whole operation."

"Forging fivers! That's class stuff!" Brian was visibly impressed. "But why not tenners? The work would be the same, but the value double."

"Good point! Fivers are as common as dirt. People seldom look twice at them. Tenners are nearly the same, but attract more attention. As for twenties, well everybody looks twice at them! We've got plates for tenners and, if the fivers get rumbled and people stop accepting them, we'll be ready to supply the demand for tenners!"

"Cor! There's a fortune to be made here!"

"Yes! Well, there's lots to be done. First we'll get the blocking press going. That way, when I don't need you to help putting the GTO together, you can be putting the silver on. The opaque white and the watermark can be done on your Solna. That way, you'll have the paper ready by the time the GTO's fit for doing the colour print."

"What about the plates?"

"All in the van," replied David with a grin. "I was working on them as soon as Harry had taken over Watsons. Harry and I go back a long way, but we reckoned it best to act as if we were meeting for the first time. All the plates were ready weeks before the auction. Just as well! The police have been round at Smithers several times, not that there's anything to find there, but it would have been tricky trying to do the plates on Smithers' premises. One of the staff might have rumbled us. Right! Now let's get on with it." And, with that, they set to with a will.

Thanks to the generous help of the Highlands and Islands Development Board, the previously sloping floor with the drainage channel running the length of the stable had been re-laid in concrete to suit the needs of the dreams of the ornamental ironwork man. David selected a suitable corner and the two of them crow-barred the big blocking press into position. It was so massive that David decided that there was no need to delay things by anchoring it down. It's own weight would ensure it did not move. Wiring it up was straightforward and, by late morning, the first sheets were being blocked. Adjustment of the temperature was largely trial and error, but it did not take long for Brian to get the hang of the machine. He loaded up the feed-board with some of the paper from the Transit and soon the machine was producing. It was old and its running speed was only about 1,500 sheets per hour. On the other hand, it settled down to chug along at this slow pace and soon Brian found he could safely turn his back on it. This left the two of them free to get on with other work. The blocking press switched itself off when the feed-board was empty, so all he had to do was to keep an eye on the reels of blocking foil, to make sure they did not run out, and to re-fill the feed board every so often.

Meanwhile, David was working on the GTO. He positioned the first unit, levelling it with great care. He checked and re-checked with a spirit level, knowing that hours of care now could save days of frustration later. When he was at last satisfied, he coupled up the second unit, carefully levelling it. This was followed by the third and then the fourth, each being secured to the concrete floor with special adhesive. It was the afternoon of the second day before he was satisfied that all was correct. The two stood in awe as they watched the first experimental batch of paper pass through at the rate of more than two sheets per second.

"Think about it, Brian my boy! Each sheet will need to go through five times, but at 8,000 sheets per hour, multiplied by ten fivers per sheet, divided by five times through: that's still 16,000 completed notes per hour. £80,000. Even allowing for plate changing, we should be knocking off half a million a day! The problem's going to be that the washing machines won't be able to keep up!"

It did not quite work out like that. The Transit was fully laden, but still had brought only 14,000 sheets, sufficient for the first £700,000 of five-pound notes. The GTO ran fast enough, but the blocking machine and the collator were much slower and so the GTO was idle for hours at a time. Nevertheless, at the end of the first full week, the two had produced £660,000, after discarding spoils and substandard work. They felt justifiably pleased with themselves.

Inevitably, there was some spoilage. By the end of the run, a considerable pile of waste had accumulated. There were partly printed sheets which David had rejected because the positioning of the colours relative to one another was wrong. Others were rejected because the shade of print was either too strong or too weak. There were also a number of single notes that had been too badly mangled around in the washing machines.

"We've got to be very careful about the waste," said David. "There was a forger in Glasgow who was caught because some fool disposed of a few of his spoilt sheets in the skip at the back of his factory. I suggested to Harry that we ship the waste out with the good notes and dump it somewhere far from here, but he wouldn't hear of it. We've to burn it all here, as if we didn't have enough to do!"

Burning the waste did take time. A large metal dustbin

with holes punched in it acted as an incinerator. An elaborate wire-mesh cover prevented any partly burnt material going up with the smoke. The big problem was that the bin was sited in the corner of the courtyard and was so well sheltered that there was not enough draught to keep the fire going. Paper is remarkably difficult stuff to burn in large quantities, especially if it is necessary to get rid of every last scrap. Soon, the waste disposal part of the operation became another serious bottle-neck in the production cycle.

Chapter 14

The washing machines did their job, but held things up badly. It was not just that they could not keep up with the Heidelberg. Loading the notes in took no time, but disentangling them from the rags etc. was a laborious job. The finished job was impressive, however. Every note looked as though it had served its country well and for many, many years. They looked the kind of thing that would make a man or woman of any refinement want to wash their hands after handling them. There was certainly no incentive to examine them in great detail.

Brian had taken a batch of his paintings into Inverness and had posted an innocent looking greeting card to Harry with a coded message that the first batch was ready for distribution. Harry was obsessed with security and never contacted his clandestine printing concern in the Highlands direct. This slowed down communication so there was a lag of two days before a large American mobile home arrived at the stable. The Highlands in the summer are awash with every conceivable variety of caravan, caravanette and mobile home. One being driven slowly by a middle-aged man in a flowery shirt accompanied by a florid middle-aged woman attracted no attention at all, even when on quiet back roads. The man rapped on the door and it was opened promptly by Brian. The vehicle was driven in and the door closed again.

"You must be Brian," said the newcomer as he climbed out

of the driving seat. "What roads! It's taken us hours to cover less than a hundred miles from Perth. The last few miles were the worst. It's no joke driving one of these mobile greenhouses on these one-track roads. We'd better move smartly. Harry wants me to book into a site near Dingwall for the night so that no one can associate this thing with Speyside. He's cranky about security."

"Don't tell me! We're living like exiles here, banned from going to pubs, discos or anything. However, it should all be worthwhile in the long run. What've you got for us?"

"More paper, for starters. A ton or more, I should think, judging by the way it held me back on the Drummochter pass! Let's unload and then let's see what you've got for me."

Working with a will, the three of them unloaded the reams of paper on to a hand-barrow and dragged it into the stable. There, in cardboard cartons of various sizes, were the bank-notes. The men paused for a tea-break between the unloading and the loading operations.

"In some ways," said Brian, "producing the money must be easier than distributing it. How does Harry intend to get rid of half a million without it being traced back to him? Even if the money was genuine, how do you spend tens of thousands in fivers without being noticed?"

"You're dead right! Getting rid of large wads of notes will always attract attention. Harry has lots of contacts and he'll sell the notes in blocks to distributors up and down the country. They, in turn, will pass them on to lesser lights and so on. Harry's right to be cautious. Some of the petty crooks at the end of the line are pretty thick. Sooner or later, one of them will be caught and'll squeal. That's when you'll be glad of Harry's obsession with security! It'll keep the likes of you and me out of the clink."

"I just hope you're right. I would like to have the chance to spend some of the loot before I get banged up!"

"Nobody'll be banged up if we're all careful. Now, let's get me loaded up and away. The shorter time I'm around here, the better."

An hour later, the mobile home was on the road, bound for Inverness and beyond. It was several days later before it passed through Carlisle. There it strayed into a run-down industrial estate and pulled into the same disused warehouse that the lorry carrying the Heidelberg had lurked in a few weeks earlier. It stayed only long enough for the cartons to be transferred to a waiting Transit. Then the middle-aged couple set off to finish their holidays with a visit to the Lake District.

Anonymous distribution was, indeed, a problem. Harry was reconciled to getting only 20p in the £1 for his notes and he was relying on the distributors to use the traditional method of laundering 'funny money', on-course betting. Anyone wishing to dispose of large quantities of forged notes can quite anonymously place bets at horse and dog races. In the heat and bustle of accepting last minute bets, bookies have no time to scrutinise every last fiver. If they accept forgeries, the chances are that they will off-load most, if not all of them, on the lucky winners before the end of the day. This means that the bookie can afford not to be too fussy as punters thrust money feverishly into his hands. Meanwhile, the pedlars of the dodgy money hope that they will win some as well as lose some. Their winnings may include some of their own forgeries, but, on average, they hope to get back more good than bad. The police were well aware of this time-honoured system and Harry took great pains to ensure there were several cut-outs between him and the lower echelons who might end up in a police cell. All in all, he felt fairly secure.

Chapter 15

As far as Inspector Flint was concerned, the trail of the missing Heidelberg had gone cold. Whilst he still entertained suspicions about Harry Robson, he could no longer even think of a credible excuse to visit Rupert Smithers and Co. There was not the slightest evidence to suggest the press had left the country. It had just vanished into thin air. Over many a pint, he discussed all the various scenarios with Alfred Reid. They came up with many an ingenious theory. The more pints, the more ingenious were the theories. However, crime did not stop simply because there was this on-going puzzle and Flint soon found himself investigating muggings, murders and rapes which had to take priority. The case of the missing Heidelberg, though not closed, was definitely on the back-burner.

Early in August, questions about printing were again to the fore. Nearly every racecourse in and around London was flooded with forged £5 notes. All looked as though they had been in circulation for months, if not years, and it was puzzling why no one had reported them before. Then reports came in from York, from Wetherby, from Doncaster, from Aintree and from another dozen race-courses up and down the country. The Bank of England was struggling to establish the pattern of the numbering of the forged notes. The difficulty was that the sequence of numbers was not readily identifiable. Any blanket condemnation of a batch of numbers condemned more good than bad. Flint waved a handful of notes in front of Reid in the snug of the Crown and Whistle.

" See what we're up against?" he said. "I dare say these would not fool you, but the man in the street would be taken in, wouldn't you say?"

Reid examined the proffered notes carefully. He pulled out a small magnifying glass and scrutinised the notes one by one. "They're good. There's no doubt but what they're good. You've twenty here and all with different numbers. Indeed, the numbers are so different that I couldn't predict what pattern they follow."

"I can't help associating them with that ruddy Heidelberg," said Flint. "Could these be printed on a machine like that? The numbering's so good that I have been told that it's printed litho, rather than with some kind of numbering machine. Any ideas?"

"It's impossible to look at a piece of printed matter and say categorically that it was produced on a particular machine or, for that matter, a particular type of machine. It is possible to say what kind of machine could not have printed it, but that's not much help. These notes could have been done on a GTO. There's no doubt about that. Even the numbering could have been printed, although it would be a laborious job, needing goodness knows how many different plates if the forger wanted to avoid having too many duplicates. The metal strip is convincing if you look at it superficially. You'll of course know that it's just foil-blocked? Anyone who really looked could tell it was not genuine if they put their mind to it. There again, who does examine used notes carefully, especially when they're as old as these?"

"Clever that, isn't it? Flint replied. "The boffins reckon they've been artificially aged. 'Distressing', I believe they call it in the antique reproduction business. You know, where a newly made piece of furniture deliberately has worm-holes and scratches added to give the appearance of being centuries old. We still have no clear picture of the sequence of numbers the forgers are using, so we can't issue warnings about them. It may take weeks before we've any idea of the scale of the scam. If it were our GTO that's printing these, have you any idea how many they could produce in a week?"

"I suppose I could make an informed guess, but, if, for instance, you can't tell me whether the machine's on an eight hour day or being run twenty-four hours a day on shift work, there's no way I could be accurate." Alfred thought for a few minutes, then he went on, "Eight hours a day, five days a week, allowing for lots of delays to change the numbering plates often? I'd say between £800,000 and £1,000,000 each week. If they are on a twenty-four hour day and a seven day week, you can multiply by four. That's an awful lot of money!" There was another long pause as he struggled with mental arithmetic. "That's a lot of paper. With a calculator, I could give you a very accurate figure, but there must be nearly a ton of paper needed to print a million pounds of fivers. Our forgers must be getting anything from a ton to four tons of paper a week from somewhere. Your best line of enquiry might be at the paper mills. Your boffins can possibly tell you which mill made the paper. These notes are so crumpled that I could not hazard a guess." He held one up to the light. "It doesn't look anything out of the ordinary, just a middle of the road smooth cartridge. Could be from any of a dozen British mills or it could be an import. Even if you narrow it down to one mill, it's the kind of stuff that's produced at the rate of hundreds of tons a week and sold through merchants. The mill will almost certainly not know who prints its paper, except, of course, for the really large users who buy direct, by-passing the merchants."

"Thanks, but it doesn't take us much further, does it? I may be on a wild goose chase so far as associating the theft of the Heidelberg with forging. Why bother stealing a press when it's first day's output would just about pay for it? It seems to me that that would just involve the police at an unnecessarily early stage."

Alfred replied thoughtfully, "No. It's perhaps not surprising. If the forger could not raise the cash to buy the press, then stealing it might be the obvious solution"

"Then that let's our Harry off the hook. He did have the money and had bought the machine. Why attract attention to himself by having it stolen?"

"Well, he could hardly have spent over £100,000 on a machine and not brought it into use. That would have attracted even more attention. His staff would ask questions, or at least gossip and speculate in the pub as to what he'd done with it. Then his accountant would want to know where it was and so would the Revenue. If he had not installed it in his factory, they'd assume he'd sold it and pocketed the proceeds without putting them through his books. Stealing it is a viable way of getting a good press that cannot be traced back to you. I'm not saying Harry Robson's done that, but I am saying he might have."

They parted shortly after. Flint felt no further forward. He was baffled and deeply depressed.

Chapter 16

After leaving his old friend, Angus, Dougal drove south towards Glasgow and his home. As he went, he found himself driving more and more slowly, dreading the moment when he would actually arrive at his empty house. It was therefore mid-afternoon when he reached his desination. He showered and changed, then set out for the bank. The manager listened sympathetically to his story.

"Well, first, we'd better get your credit cards cancelled," he said.

"I suppose so," replied Dougal. "Although only a deep-sea diver's going to find them now! My cheque book went down with the boat. Is there any problem about issuing a new one?"

"None at all. I'm sure we'll have one ready here so you can pick it up on your way out. May I congratulate you on your escape! I don't know whether this is the right time to mention it, but if you're thinking of replacing your yacht, the bank will be very happy to help with finance, should you require a loan."

Dougal grinned. "Give me time to recover my insanity!" he said. "Right now I'm suffering from an unusual attack of common-sense and am vowing never to get in a boat again. Don't worry, it'll wear off! When it does, I'll probably be back here cap in hand."

He picked up the new cheque book and left the bank feeling a little more comfortable, having got that bit of business out of the way. The first thing he did when he reached home was to write to Mr and Mrs Morris, thanking them for all their kindness and returning the loan. As evening came on, the loneliness of the house seemed to close in on Dougal. The high brought on by the excitement and action of the last few days evaporated and a black depression fell like a fog around him. He started drinking beer with a little whisky added. By bed-time, he was drinking whisky with a little beer added. Eventually, scarcely able to stand, he staggered off to bed and collapsed on to it still fully dressed.

The following morning, he awoke with a raging thirst and a splitting head-ache. He cursed himself for being a fool and drank mug after mug of tea. It was lunch-time before he felt like eating and, even then, he could only face a light snack. He could not go on like this, he knew, but what was he to do? Part of him wanted to move house, to run away from everything that reminded him of happier times, everything that reminded him of Stella. Another part of him could not face up to change at all. Indecision was easier than decisive action. Yet another and more rational part said, "Don't do anything drastic while you're depressed. You'll only regret it later." This, he knew, would be the kind of advice he would get if he sought bereavement counselling. But what if he stayed permanently depressed? When would be the right time to make a move? How long would this inner pain go on for? "Time is a great healer," a sympathetic friend had said after Stella's funeral. But how much time? The ache of his loss seemed, if anything, worse now than in the first stunned days of being alone. Thoughts of ending it all surged up afresh. To live or to die? Or should it be 'To die or to live?'

Forcing himself, he looked out a road atlas and tried to plan what to do with the remaining four weeks of holiday.

If he stayed at home, he would end up a suicide or a mental patient. With no yacht, he hardly knew what to do. It was while he was doing this that he came upon the envelope that he had misappropriated at the old manse at Kinloch Esk. He opened it and read the terse note inside.

"Rod Finlay picked up a clue to the whereabouts of Harry's printing operation. 'Altnariach'. Sounds Scottish but I cannot trace it. Any ideas? Be careful where you spend any of those fivers. Tennant"

Dougal was puzzled. 'Altnariach' rang a very vague bell in his memory. He was sure he had seen the name before but could not place it. Somehow it reminded him of Aviemore and the Cairngorms, but he could not work out the connection. There was 'Braeriach', of course, one of the four highest peaks of the Cairngorm range. He had climbed it more than once. That reminded him of 'Inschriach', part of the Rothiemurchas Forest. That was near Aviemore and might explain the tie-up in his mind linking 'Altnariach' and Aviemore.

Then Dougal thought about the fivers. He hauled out the rucksack and pulled out a wad on the grubby notes it contained. They looked genuine enough, but the warning to take care with spending them plus the reference to printing made him examine them with greater care. He was no expert, but he came to the conclusion they must be forgeries. He, too, would have to be careful!

None of this helped him with his own immediate problems and how to tackle them. What was he going to do and where was he going to go? Eventually, he took two decisions. First, he would go north. He would find a bed and breakfast and tramp the Cairngorms. He could also keep an eye open for 'Altnariach'. Rather reluctantly, he admitted to himself that the adrenalin rush arising from his recent adventures had given those few days a sparkle that had been missing in his life. Hunting down a forger's hidden printing press might again bring some exitement and help to take his mind off his own depressed state. If he had seen

'Altnariach' on a previous trip, he might well stumble on it again. The second decision was to shave off his beard. That was a difficult decision to take. His beard had served him well during his recent adventures but the fact that it was by far his most distinctive feature might mean that the word had gone out amongst the drug-runners' friends to track down a tall man with a black beard. Shaving it off was like parting with an old friend, but Dougal had to admit he scarcely recognised the young man who stared back at him when he looked in the mirror. Shaving had knocked at least ten years off his appearance.

That evening, he went for a long walk and managed to get to bed without drinking a drop. The next morning, he felt the better for it. He packed a rucksack and loaded it into his Escort. By lunch-time, he was in Kingussie, ten miles south of Aviemore and close to Glen Feshie, his jumping off point for the Cairngorms. He found a comfortable bed and breakfast guest house and then spent the afternoon with his binoculars in the marshes of the Spey bird-watching. The black cloud of depression lifted as suddenly as it had fallen and he felt relaxed and happy.

The following day dawned bright, though with clouds forming in the west. Dougal made an early start and by 9am had parked his car at the head of the public road up Glen Feshie. He slung his rucksack on his back and strode off east-wards, climbing steadily into the Cairngorms. The path took him over the shoulder of Carn Ban Mor and on to the massive Cairn Toul which towered to more than 4,000 feet. Patchy cloud and mist obscured his view of Ben Macdui to the east, across the steep-sided pass known as Lairig Ghru. To the north lay Cairn Toul's sister peak, Braeriach, another summit over 4,000 feet above sea-level. He had plenty of time and felt fine, so he decided to take in Braeriach on his way back. The peaks were only two and a half miles apart as the crow, or, in this terrain, as the eagle flies. The route on foot round the ridge did, in fact, double this. For all that, it was easy going and, except for a few spots of rain, the weather remained dry.

After Braeriach, it all changed. Black clouds loomed and the rain was soon battering down. Dougal pulled on his cagoule and kept his head down. Soon he was navigating by compass alone. His clothes kept him almost totally dry, but he was glad when, in late afternoon, he reached Glen Feshie and his waiting car. By the time he reached Kingussie, his legs had stiffened up, but he felt cheered by the sense of achievement. That night the rain fell in torrents. The mountain streams rose rapidly. The following day saw no improvement in the weather. Dougal stayed in, relaxed and read. As the rain eased off in the evening, he went out and re-visited the marshes. The Spey had risen and the floods covered even more of the plain than they had a couple of days before.

Chapter 17

That night Dougal slept fitfully, possibly because he was simply not tired enough. The next day was a little brighter, although it looked as if it would continue to be showery. Dougal felt he simply must get out and, as the sky looked slightly lighter in the northeast, he drove off in that direction. Showers came and went. He stopped once or twice and walked, never going far from the car. At a village inn he stopped for a pub lunch. As he came out, a glimmer of sunlight blinked through the clouds. He strolled through the village and down to the raging stream that cascaded under the bridge. He leant over the parapet, deep in depression. These mood-swings were alarming. He had run away from home, but his problems still dogged his footsteps. Miserably, he gazed down into the swirling pool far below and the water being channelled into a four foot gap at the far side. Beyond that was a water-fall, not itself visible but evident from the spray that rose like smoke above it. Morosely, he gazed unseeingly down. He was oblivious to the comings and goings of tourists and others around him, as he stayed there, propped up on the parapet.

Suddenly, from his left, there came a cry. He swung round in time to see child overbalance and tumbled head-first into the river below. Almost before the kid hit the water, Dougal was air-borne, something between a dive and a jump, and he was plummeting into the pool twenty feet below. As his body arced through the air, he glimpsed another body, falling parallel to his own. He hit the surface badly with a great splash. This did have the merit that he did not go down deep. In seconds, he had surfaced and two strong strokes had him within reach of the child. As he grabbed the kid from one side, another figure surfaced on the other and also gripped the youngster. Together, the rescuers started to swim for the bank, pulling the inert body behind them. However, the current gripped them and, despite their combined efforts, all three were drawn inexorably nearer and nearer the fall. Dougal put in one last tremendous effort, swimming with all his remaining strength for safety. It was useless. Foot by foot, the current drew them on. The noise of the fall was now deafening. It was a losing battle and the three were suddenly thrust violently through the gap and hurled into the abyss below.

Dougal landed and, a micro-second later, the other two crashed down on top of him. The next few seconds were a tumultuous nightmare of water, noise and pain. Somehow, he maintained his grasp of the child's clothing. He was bashed off rocks to both left and right. His head banged off the bottom. The water calmed for a moment, but only before plunging over another fall. As he fell over this, Dougal felt his right leg catch. The current yanked at his body and, despite the roar of water all around him, he heard a bone snap like a carrot.

Then, all was calm. He was under the water and the current still swept him along, but the force had eased. He tried to swim and all but passed out as a wave of pain shot from his leg and seemed to embrace his whole body. He tried to fight his way to the surface and failed. His lungs were at bursting point. Why did he bother to fight it? Had he not been seeking death only, up to now, to find it eluded him? All he had to do was to relax and he would find a hero's grave. He was blacking out. Consciousness ebbed and flowed. Then suddenly his head broke the surface. He gulped half a lungful of air before going down again. This time he surfaced sooner, not sure if he was glad he was still alive or not.

He was being swept down a comparatively calm stretch of river. A voice in his ear said, "Why can't you swim on the top of the water like everyone else?" He swung round and saw a face only eighteen inches from his own. It barely registered before he was sucked down again. "Why don't you swim on the top of the water like everyone else?" What kind of a fool question was that at a time like this? Suddenly he wanted to meet the idiot who asked it. The will to survive surged through him. He kicked out with his good leg and surfaced again.

The river levelled out and became progressively calmer. The three clung to together and a back-water seized them, sweeping them under some trees. Dougal grabbed a branch with his free hand. The others surged past him, checked and then swung in an arc on to the shore at a gravel beach. Dougal held on until he could see they were securely ashore, then he let go. His good foot found the bottom and he half walked, half crawled out of the water. The child was unconscious. Gasping for breath himself, Dougal rolled the small body on to its back. He took in the fact that this was a boy even as he groped round the kid's neck to feel for a pulse. Nothing! Painfully, he pulled himself up over the prostrate figure. He pushed the heel of his hand into the lad's chest and found the point where the rib cage ended. He eased back, thrust the heel of his hand down, counted to ten and repeated the exercise. As he leant over the kid, big drops of blood dripped from his head on to the unconscious form.

Meanwhile the other swimmer pulled the boy's head back firmly, nipped his nose and, mouth-to-mouth, breathed steadily into the kid's lungs. For what seemed an eternity, there was no sign of life. Then the boy coughed and stirred. Dougal stopped the heart massage. He wiped back his sodden hair and looked dazed at the blood on his hand. He knew he had hit his head more than once and wondered what on earth he must look like, covered in blood like this. His companion turned and grinned. It was only then he realised that this was a woman. She was no beauty and indeed, with her hair tangled and matted down her face, she looked like some sea-monster. That was until she smiled. That smile lit up her whole face.

Like Dougal, she was still breathless but she gasped, "We've done it! Thank God, we've done it!" Then rescued and rescuers lay exhausted on the shingle. The two adults pressed their bodies against the child in some kind of surreal sandwich with the kid as the filling. Looking over the youngster's tousled head, their eyes met.

"When we've got this kid warmed up," the woman said, "I'll stay with him and you go for help."

"No, I'll stay with him and you go for help," replied Dougal, by now faint with the pain in his leg.

"You'll have to go. I'm sorry, but I've broken my arm and I don't know if I can get up that bank and over the fence." She nodded behind him at the near-vertical bank that rose from where they lay and was topped fifty feet higher up by a barbed-wire fence.

"I've bust my leg," Dougal gasped. The result was totally unexpected. The face before him crumpled up in laughter. Her laughter was infectious and, despite his pain, Dougal found himself joining in.

"I'm sorry, laughing like that," she said, trying, not very successfully, to look serious. "I wasn't laughing at you, honestly. It's just such a ridiculous situation. Both of us crocks! Well! What do we do now? Just wait and hope someone comes looking for us? Was anyone with you?"

"No! No one will miss me," said Dougal with some feeling. "How about you?"

"I was alone too. We'll just have to hope that someone saw

or that there was someone with this kid, otherwise we're in for a long wait!"

It was a long wait, or at least it seemed that to Dougal. In the event, it was less than half an hour later that a voice above them made them both look up. Looking over the fence was a policeman. He scrambled agilely over the fence and slithered down to where they lay. He grasped the situation at once. He spoke rapidly into his radio which squawked back in reply.

"Doctor's on his way. Helicopter's scrambled." This was obviously the strong, silent type of copper. There was no attempt at further conversation until a tall, young man with a bag appeared above them and struggled down to join them.

"Lady's arm's broken. Man's leg too. Kid's fine," said the laconic bobby.

The doctor eased the pressure from the woman's arm. He hung it in a sling, rolled up her sleeve and gave her a shot from a hypodermic. He gave the boy a cursory once-over, but the kid was obviously only shaken. Then he came to Dougal. With smooth professionalism, he straightened the broken limb. Dougal winced. "Mmm. Bad break that. I'll give you something for the pain. The helicopter's on its way. You just lie still and we'll have you in hospital before you know it."

Dougal felt the needle puncture his arm, then everything seemed to drift away. He was floating. The woman's face came and went, came and went, the woman who laughed at a broken arm. It came and went, this time not to return. "And I don't even know her name," was his last conscious thought.

Chapter 18

Dougal was struggling to walk on his crutches. The last few days had been a nightmare of pain. His leg was badly fractured and the broken ends of the bone had been ground against each other as he had hurtled through the rapids. There was even a point when the orthopaedic surgeon was having to consider the possibility of amputation. However, a long operation had put three steel pins in his leg and he had been assured that, in due time, he would be perfectly fit again. The hospital staff had been great and he was very grateful for all that had been done for him. The rescue had been widely reported in the newspapers and on television but, at the crucial time, Dougal was in the operating theatre and not available for interview. The media had therefore made a heroine of his co-rescuer. The result was that, by the time he might have been fit enough to see reporters, the whole matter, inevitably, was yesterday's news and so he was left in peace. This, with his recent exploits at Kinloch Esk in mind, was a great relief. Having his picture and name and address splashed across the papers was the last thing he wanted.

There had been an ugly moment in the ward not long after he had been admitted. He had been lying in a heavily sedated state when two policemen went up the ward and returned escorting a patient. The man did not even give Dougal a glance, which was just as well, for it was his former captor, the man whom Dougal had shot in the thigh. Whether the man would have recognised Dougal with no beard, he could not guess. Had the distinctive black adornment still been there on his face, it might well have caught the fellow's eye.

At visiting times, Dougal did feel his isolation. Other patients were surrounded by almost excessive numbers of caring relatives and friends, whilst he had no one. At these times, he buried himself in a book and tried hard not to get depressed. The bouts of depression still came, but possibly were not so deep and passed more quickly. Certainly, his obsessive thinking about death and suicide was less prevalent. He worked very hard with the physiotherapists and was determined to get out as soon as possible. At the back of his mind, however, was a positive dread of returning to the empty house at Blackgorge.

As he stumped along the ward on the unfamiliar crutches, he saw a woman coming towards him, her arm in a sling. She looked totally different when her blond hair was not soaked and straggling over her face, but he would have recognised her anywhere. Kathleen Browning. He had got her name from the newspaper report. She was slim to the point of being unhealthily thin and certainly no classical beauty, but, as she walked towards him, her face was transformed with an electrifying smile.

"Hi! So you're on your feet, then? I looked in twice before but both times you were out for the count and it seemed a shame to wake you. I've come to say goodbye. I'm being discharged but I did want to say hello before I went. Do you think you can make it to the cafe for a cup of coffee?"

Dougal had mixed emotions. A wave of gratitude swept over him. He suddenly realised how much he had been longing for a friendly visitor. No matter how friendly and helpful the hospital staff had been, [and they had been superb], he had yearned for someone to talk to. With the gratitude came disappointment. She had come to say goodbye. Perhaps it was just as well. Emotionally, he was a mess and this was no time to get involved at any level with a woman. He took in the fact that she wore a wedding ring. If she was someone else's wife, it might be best if they parted almost as soon as they met. He felt this all the more acutely because there was an undeniable magnetism about this woman. He could not define it. It certainly was not physical beauty and equally not sex-appeal. Something to do with personality, with character, with empathy. Whatever it was, it defied definition. With these thoughts tumbling through his head, Dougal hobbled his way along the corridor beside her. He was feeling like a tongue-tied teenager, wondering what to say which would not sound banal. Fortunately, she was far from tongue-tied.

"I came to Scotland for peace and quiet! You've no idea what a cross-examination I've had from the press. They ask such stupid questions. 'Was I glad to have been there at the right time? What was the water like?' I ask you! 'What was the water like!' How inane can they get? I just said,' Wet!' And, do you know this? The great big dumpling thought I was being serious! Where do they find these people? You know this? I found myself praying for an earthquake, or at least some juicy sexual scandal in high society, anything to get that lot off my back! But look, I'm sorry. Here's me babbling on about my petty troubles and you're the real hero. How is your leg? They told me it was quite badly smashed. What about your head, too? That's a very impressive bandage, you know." She stopped, looked at him and grinned.

Then she went on, "You know, there was a moment when I thought we'd all had it. We were belting down the rapids and I thought we'd all be smashed to bits or drown. Then I saw you. The blood was pouring down your face. It looked far worse than it really was, no doubt. A little blood goes a long way when you mix it with water. You had such a look of dogged determination on your face and you were so obviously putting all you had into swimming that I just knew you'd get us through safely! I was at the point of giving up but that gave me new strength."

If you only knew, thought Dougal. If you only knew how nearly I came to throwing in the towel. It was only that stupid question, 'Why don't you swim on top of the water like everyone else?' I wanted to see who could ask something so daft and that kept me going.

Out loud he said, "I'm fine thanks. Of course, my leg hurts, but so does almost everything else. You must be the same, bruised and battered from head to toe!"

"Too true. I looked at myself in a full-length mirror and said, 'There you are, my girl! That's you in glorious technicolour! Every conceivable shade of yellow, blue and black! I never believed I could turn out to be such a colourful character! Seriously, though, the arm aches a bit and the plaster makes me itch, but it's really nothing. The laugh of it is that you and I got knocked all over the place yet there's hardly a mark on the kid. I think you and I must have cushioned him all the way through the rocks. I certainly feel as if I did! He was discharged the next day and his folk have taken him back to Manchester. They all came to see you before they left to say thanks but you were so heavily sedated that I don't imagine you'll remember. They'll no doubt write to you. They were really very grateful, although they weren't half angry at the kid. I just hope they don't give him too hard a time. It wasn't as if he meant to fall!"

They had reached the cafe by now. Kathleen insisted Dougal sit down while she rather awkwardly, using only her one good arm, bought coffee and biscuits. When she had settled down at the table, she asked, "Have they told you when you'll be able to leave?"

"Not in so many words, but I think they'll want me out in a couple of days or so. I suppose I'll be able to go home by train. I certainly won't be driving for a while. The police picked up my car for me and they say it can live in their compound for as long as I like, so I've no problems there."

"Does your wife not drive then?" She asked.

Dougal blinked. "What makes you think that I'm married?"

"Well, you are aren't you," she replied with a triumphant twinkle in her eye. "It shows! Any reasonably sensitive woman knows within a very short time if a chap's married and, in not much more time, whether he's happily married. Oh dear! What have I said?"

A tear formed unbidden in Dougal's eye. He looked away. Then he said with brutal brevity, "Yes, I was married, happily married, but my wife's dead."

"Oh! What a stupid, vain, insensitive idiot I am! I'm sorry. I'm so sorry. I was so cocky about being able to guess. I'm usually right, but I've been so stupid this time! Why can't I keep my big mouth shut!"

Dougal looked up, "It's all right. It's really all right. It's just that it's all so recent that I've not fully taken it in. Please just forget this whole conversation."

There was a protracted, awkward silence. Then, to break it, Dougal asked, "Tell me about yourself. Where are you from and what do you do?"

"North London. I'm a civilian employee of the Metropolitan police. I'm staying with an aunt in Inverness who runs a small guest house. I'm going back south on the night train. There are things I've to see to back home. After that, well, I'm just not sure. Where is it you're from?"

"Glasgow, or, more precisely, a grotty suburb of Glasgow called Blackgorge. It's on the east side. I teach in the local school."

"And is there anyone to look after you when you go

home," she asked.

"No, but there again, I don't need anyone. I can look after myself."

"It's just that I was thinking that, if you like, I could fix it with my aunt for you to get my room at the guesthouse after I leave. That way, you wouldn't have to make the train journey until you're a bit better and you'll be able to attend out-patients and physiotherapy here rather than at some other hospital in Glasgow. How's that sound?"

It sounded good. Dougal realised just how much he had been dreading returning home, knowing he would be a virtual prisoner in his own house for some considerable time until his leg healed.

Chapter 19

Dougal was discharged from hospital four days after he had said his goodbyes to Kathleen. She had cheered up a bit, but was still remorseful when she left. He tried to put her out of his mind, but found himself coming back to their conversation again and again. Although she appeared to do most of the talking, he realised that she had drawn out far more about him than he had learned about her. This was undoubtedly due, at least in part, to the fact that she was much more interested in learning about him than he was about her. She was another man's wife, even if she was downright evasive when he made an oblique reference to her husband. Quite apart from that, he did not want any kind of romantic entanglement, still less an affair with a married woman. He determined, therefore, to show no more than a polite interest in her when he went to her aunt's guest-house. Her aunt, a Mrs Dryden, was a fussy, little woman in her sixties. She bustled around and seemed always in a hurry. Conversations with her were few and brief, a fact that suited Dougal admirably.

About a week into his stay at the guest-house, she announced that Kathleen would be coming north again at the weekend.

"Poor dear, she's doing so well considering," she muttered, more to herself than to Dougal. He longed to ask, "Considering what?" but thought it best to say nothing. Nevertheless, Mrs Dryden saw the look of enquiry on his face.

"Please forget I said that. She asked me not to talk about herself with you."

"That's all right. We all have things we like to keep to ourselves. I'll listen to anything she wants to tell me, but I won't pry, so don't you worry."

Kathleen arrived early on the Saturday morning, having come north on the London to Inverness sleeper. She looked exhausted and, after breakfasting, disappeared into her room. It was late afternoon before she emerged, looking tired and drawn. Dougal was deep into a novel and hardly noticed when she entered the resident's lounge.

She came over to the corner where he sat. "Hi! How goes it? The leg getting better?"

"Oh! Fine, thanks. I'm sorry, I didn't notice you there. Would you like to sit down?" He gestured to the next arm-chair. She sank into it, turned and smiled.

"You're looking so much better. You had a right prison pallor when I last saw you. I see you've lost the head bandage. Has that all cleared up?" she asked.

"Yes, thanks. It was more of a graze than a cut. A piece of skin was scraped right off. That's why there was so much blood. Of course, these things always tend to look much worse than they really are. How are you? I see you're still in plaster. When do you think you'll get that off?"

"Monday, with any luck. I'm due in out-patients at ten. I think they'll take it off. It feels right now. The other aches and pains are all gone. I hope you're the same?"

"Yes, thanks. The bruising has almost completely disappeared and the pain has gone completely. Are you back here for long?" asked Dougal, more for the sake of something to say than out of personal interest.

"Don't really know. Perhaps a week or two. It depends. I'll

115

decide as time goes by. At the minute, I've not made up my mind. I'm sorry. I'm keeping you from your book. I must do some shopping. Is there anything you need? I'll be delighted to shop for you."

Dougal thought for a minute. There were a number of things he was running short of and he was glad not to have to struggle in and out of shops on his crutches. He gave her a list of toiletries and other items he wanted. As Dougal handed over a couple of crumpled five-pound notes, he felt a pang of guilt. The only money he had left was half a dozen of the suspect fivers. After she had left, Dougal reflected that it was rather nice to have someone like Kathleen around. That she was married was a good thing. He could hope to have intelligent conversation with her and a casual friendship without wondering all the time if she thought he was trying to get off with her.

Chapter 20

As August drifted by, Dougal found himself comfortably content to stay in Inverness. He had written to the Education Authority and to the headmaster at Blackgorge High and had forecast his return to teaching as being after the autumn holidays. As the strength came back to his leg, the crutches were replaced by a walking stick. He still did not feel ready to resume driving and so his Escort remained in the compound at the police headquarters.

September began with magnificently sunny days but also with something of an autumn chill. Dougal began to realise that he would have to face up to going home, if only to pick up warm clothing. During this period, Kathleen came and went. She would stay for a week or so, then go back to London for a few days. She did not volunteer any information about herself and Dougal did not ask. When she was there, they spent lazy days strolling along the walks beside the River Ness and evenings playing chess or watching television. The undemanding companionship suited Dougal's mood well, although he was dimly aware that he was going to miss her friendship when he did go home. He had picked up a train timetable and was working out how best to go back to Blackgorge, when Kathleen entered the sitting room.

"Thinking of leaving us, are you?" she enquired.

"I'll have to sooner or later, but not just yet. I'm thinking of a day-trip home to make sure everything's all right back at my flat. I must pick up some more clothes now it's getting cooler. I don't feel like driving so it'll have to be the train."

"Would you like me to drive you down? If you don't mind a stranger driving your car, we could make a day's outing of it and it'll be a lot easier for you to carry your clothes in the car than the train."

"No, no. I can't put you to so much trouble. It's very kind of you to offer, but I'll take the train."

"Look! I wouldn't have offered if it was too much trouble. Why don't we go and pick up your car and you can assess my driving and, if you think your nerves will stand it, I'll be your chauffeur!"

Dougal protested feebly, but ended up going to the compound and reclaiming his car. He drove it out himself but soon found that the driving posture gave him cramp in his bad leg. It would clearly be some time before he could drive any great distance himself and so he accepted Kathleen's offer. In the event she showed herself to be a very competent driver and he was soon totally relaxed as he left her to do the driving. The trip to Blackgorge was not particularly urgent and, as the weather continued to be exceptionally good, the pair spent the next few days exploring the countryside around Inverness.

Chapter 21

Harry had a visitor. A black Rolls Royce pulled up outside Rupert Smithers & Co. and two men got out of the front doors. They looked up and down the street, then one of them opened the rear door and a stout middle-aged man pulled himself out. He rolled across the pavement and in the door .

"Harry, old son! How goes it! Business good? I always knew you'd do well. Like I said to your old uncle, 'Where there's muck, there's brass!' Well, you've done all right pedalling your muck, but now a little bird's told me you're branching out into better quality printing. I thought you would like a partner so I've come to offer my services."

"Hello, Mr Tennant. I'm fine, but I'm not sure what you mean. Smithers are doing quite well, but I do not need or want a partner."

"I think you know perfectly well what I have in mind. Your other business is what I was thinking about. Come on, now. There's room enough for both of us and I've far better channels for distribution than you. A partnership will leave you free to produce and me and my boys to distribute."

"I'm not wanting a partnership. I'm perfectly happy the way things are, thank you." Harry replied. He certainly did not want to get involved with the likes of Jimmy Tennant. Harry had his standards. Tennant's fortunes were built up on extortion, prostitution and pornography certainly, and also, probably, on drugs. This was what unsubstantiated rumour said. Harry had done well on soft-porn, but there was no way Harry would handle anything to do with animals or children. Tennant had no such scruples. He ruled his empire with a rod of iron. In fairness, those who served with unquestioning obedience prospered. However, Harry did not want to give that kind of loyalty to such a man.

"I'm sorry, Harry. I've failed to make myself clear. If you don't want a partnership, I'll have to arrange a take-over. Tell you what, think it over. It'll be the making of you. I'll see myself out. I'll be back next week and we can have another chat." He turned and went to the door. "Let's say Tuesday, shall we? About eleven in the morning suit you? See you then." And he left.

This was an unforeseen problem for Harry. He had few principles, but he was not going to become one of Tennant's lackeys. Harry's business might be illegal and leave him liable to a lengthy prison sentence if he were caught, but he had never stooped to violence. He was a business man supplying a ready market. The punters coughed up willingly and he reckoned that he was doing no one any harm. Tennant was a different animal altogether. His fortunes were built on human misery. Each year, his drugs took their toll. Young girls were pressed into his brothels. Frightened ethnic minorities paid hefty 'insurance premiums' to ensure that their business premises did not suffer fire or vandalism and that their families escaped personal injuries. Harry wanted no part in that. There were three tons of notes stock-piled in Speyside. Distribution of tenners hadn't even started. Harry had been waiting for Government warnings about the fivers before releasing them. That night he drove north. At dawn he was at the stables and conferring with Brian and David.

"Let's take our stock of money and let him get on with it," Harry said. "If we once join forces with Tennant we'll be his serfs for life."

"But we're only just getting into the swing of things," protested David. "Give us another month and we'll have all the money we need"

"I don't know if I can buy that much time, but I'll try. I'll get another couple of tons of paper here by tomorrow evening. Work all the hours you can and we'll see what we can do before Tuesday. I'll work out something about warehousing the notes and we'll worry about distribution later. I'm getting out, but there's no need for you to get out with me. You can work for Tennant if you like."

"Let's take time to think about it," said David. "Brian and I'll get cracking and produce all we can. That'll give us room to manoeuvre. You'd better get some shut-eye."

Brian and David set about running the blocking press, [which added the silver line to the blank paper], the Solna, [which printed the water-mark and the opaque white over parts of the silver line] and the GTO, keeping all three machines going flat out on a sixteen hour day. They stopped the final operations of cutting the sheets of ten down to single notes and the washing machining, arguing that these could be done at some future date.

By midnight on Monday, the pair were exhausted, but so was the stock of unprinted paper.

Chapter 22

Dougal and Kathleen had slipped into a comfortable routine of making frequent day trips from Inverness, sometimes east along the coast to a succession of picturesque fishing villages, sometimes north to the beautiful but more bleak scenery overlooking the North Sea, sometimes westwards by Loch Ness and the stunning glens of Affric, Cannich and a dozen others. One day-trip took them south to Aviemore. There, they turned off the main road and headed into the foot-hills of the Cairngorm Mountain range, to Loch Morlich and then through the wild forests of Rothiemurchus. It was on one of these backroads that Dougal suddenly noticed they were passing a tumble-down gateway with a weather-beaten name-plate proclaiming 'Altnariach'. He was so taken aback that he nearly remarked on it, but remembered in time that he could not afford to get started on the tale that would explain his interest in it, so he held his peace. At least he now knew where it was and he could return on his own at some future date.

It was not until the last week of September that they set off for Blackgorge on a beautiful sunny day. The first autumn tints added colour to the countryside. At that time of year, the tourist traffic with its slow caravans was largely over and they made good time down the road to Glasgow. As they drew near Blackgorge, Dougal could feel depression falling on him like a dark cloud. He had been so happy here with Stella. Now he could barely face returning to the home they had shared. Kathleen followed him into the house and remained in the front room while he gathered together the various bits and pieces he had come for. She could sense his reluctance to linger and they were soon back in the car and leaving Blackgorge behind.

"You miss her dreadfully, "Kathleen said, as she saw out of the corner of her eye that Dougal's eyes were welling with tears. "Would you like to tell me about her?"

A long silence followed. Just when she was thinking she had really put her foot in it this time, Dougal began to speak, awkwardly at first, then with greater freedom. He described Stella, her looks, her personality, how they met, their shared experiences, their shared dreams. Then he haltingly went on to tell of how those dreams were shattered by her failing health. He could not bring himself to talk about their final days together and so he lapsed into silence. The silence continued for four or five miles. Then Kathleen spoke.

"It must be terrible to watch someone you love waste away and die. I had no warning of my husband's death. He went out one morning and the first thing I knew that anything was wrong was when two policewomen came to the door to tell me he had been killed outright in a motorway pile-up. I couldn't believe it at first. He was so fit and strong. Then the cruelty of it hit me. John had been in the army and, for years, I had lived with the anxiety of knowing he was in Northern Ireland or Kuwait or Bosnia. Then he was discharged and we were to be together without these enforced separations. We were going to live without the fear of him being shot or blown to pieces. He enrolled in the police and had started his training. He was in a police car that was sent to a motorway accident. The car stopped and they were just getting out when a lorry piled into them and several others smashed into it. Then the whole lot caught fire. They wouldn't let me see John's body. Perhaps that made it harder to believe he was dead. Certainly, for weeks after, I found myself expecting him to walk through the door. When the reality of it did hit me, I had a break-down. I was suicidal and, if I had remotely believed that death would have reunited us, I would have killed myself gladly. I'm signed off as fit by the doctor now, but I've taken leave of absence from my work until I'm sure I can stand the pace of returning to full-time work."

"Oh! I'm so sorry," murmured Dougal "I had no idea! I had imagined your trips south were to see your husband. It must have been terrible for you."

"No. My trips south are to see my father. He loved John from the moment they met and welcomed him as the son he had never had but had always wanted. He was shattered by John's death. Perhaps even more than he had been by my mum's. It was so unexpected and so dreadful. Over the past year dad's gone down hill terribly. He's now in a home but he's so wandered he does not really know where he is. More recently, he's completely forgotten the accident and talks to me as if John were still alive. It's awful trying to avoid his questions about how John is, why he doesn't visit and so on. I feel I must keep visiting, but these last two or three times, I've found it nearly unbearable."

Dougal did not know what to say and so he said nothing. They drove on in silence past Perth and northwards towards Inverness. When they reached Kingussie, at Dougal's suggestion they stopped for a high tea. Afterwards, they drove across the River Spey and strolled through the bird sanctuary at the Spey marshes. It was an idyllic evening. The last rays of September sunshine were still glinting over the mountains to the west, high-lighting the gaunt ruins of the Ruthven Barracks, a stark reminder of the Highland's turbulent history. Together, they walked noiselessly along the well-trodden paths and watched the varied birdlife that brought such colour and vitality to the place. Then Kathleen's eye was drawn by a scrap of paper caught in some long grass. She stooped and picked it up. It was only a scrap, perhaps two inches by three inches, with all the edges charred.

"Dougal! Look at this!" Excitedly she thrust it in front of him. He was taken aback at her sudden enthusiasm for a piece of litter. "Look!" She went on. "It's a fiver! Or, rather, part of one!"

"Someone with money to burn? Let's see." He took the fragment and examined it. A five pound note, he thought, until he turned it over. The back was blank! Immediately he knew exactly where it had come from. 'Altnariach' could only be a mile or so away, somewhere out of sight beyond the ridge to the north-east. He could not reveal his knowledge and had to act as though he were mystified.

"Now how does a partially printed bank-note come to be fluttering in the breeze in a remote bird sanctuary," he mused.

"We're on to something!" Kathleen was now really excited. "Last time I was down south, I looked in at the office. The big story there was forgery on a massive scale, with first class fivers being passed here and there all over the country. My boss has been detailed to set up a special unit. They're working all the hours there are, but have no idea where the forgeries are coming from. So far, they've lifted one or two petty crooks with fairly large sums of the stuff on them, but they're nowhere near getting to the source. I didn't like to tell you, but both fivers you gave me for your shopping were duds. I don't suppose you remember where you got them?"

Dougal remembered all too well, but he was not about to share his criminal past with Kathleen. He mutely shook his head.

She went on enthusiastically, "Don't you see? This may mean that the printing is being done somewhere near here. They are bound to spoil some and then they would have to destroy them. My guess is that this scrap escaped from a bonfire. Now, where do you think it will have come from?"

They looked around. To the west were the marshes, bogs and pools dotted with the white plumage of swans and other birds. Through the middle, the Spey meandered its leisurely way northwards. Beyond, as the ground rose on the far side of the broad valley, were a smattering of typical Highland crofts, farms and cottages, with the village of Kingussie itself at the southern end. To the south and to the north, the valley of the Spey was flat and marshy, with very few buildings of any sort. To the east, the ground rose more steeply and several farms and houses of varying size could either be seen or their presence deduced by the haze of blue wood-smoke drifting up in the still evening air.

"It seems unbelievable that a place like this could be the centre of some major criminal activity," said Dougal. "But that paper was not brought here. It must have been carried by the wind. It's not been here long. Although the weather has been dry these last few days, there's always a heavy dew at night and yet the paper seems unaffected. I would guess it's only been here for a couple of days at the most. There's no wind this evening, but there is usually some kind of light breeze so it could have come some distance and it may not have blown directly to this spot,"

"I doubt if it has come across from the west side of the valley," replied Kathleen. "It seems unlikely that it would blow past all the pools and past the river itself without getting wet. It might have done, but I think it's more probable that it originated from somewhere to the east. Look, it's going to be dark in an hour. Let's come back tomorrow and see what we can discover."

"We'd better tell the police, don't you think," asked Dougal cautiously.

"I'll phone my boss in the morning and post the thing to him. He'll take me more seriously than the locals might. Besides, everyone back at the office has been so kind to me that I owe it to them if there's a chance that they can get the credit for solving this one."

The two of them returned to Inverness and spent the rest of the evening poring over the relevant Ordnance Survey maps of the area, Kathleen trying to guess the most promising buildings to investigate, Dougal desperately trying not to draw her attention too obviously to 'Altnariach'.

Chapter 23

On the dot of 11am on the Tuesday, the black Rolls Royce swept noiselessly up to the door of Rupert Smithers office. Harry was unsurprised. If Jimmy Tennant said he was coming, he would come, sure as fate. This time there was no cordial smile or greeting from Tennant. The man was in a black fury.

"Harry, one of my boy's up in Manchester did a big cash deal at the weekend. £75,000! And every quid paid in used fivers! Every single one of them a Harry Robson production! Now I'm not blaming you personally, but you can see my problem. All my businesses are run on a strictly cash-only basis. Neither the punters, the suppliers, the girls nor I want cheques, credit cards or anything else that's traceable. But if there are going to be large quantities of funny money floating around, I'm going to be stuck with it time and time again. It just won't do! You do see where I'm coming from, now, don't you, Harry?"

Harry saw all too well. A week ago he was being offered a partnership, but now he was facing an ultimatum. This situation was not altogether unexpected. However, he did not want to appear to give in without a struggle.

"Mr Tennant, I've every sympathy. However, as you say, your recent misfortune was not my fault. It may, indeed, be an unsolicited testimonial to the quality of what I have to offer. I certainly do not want any ill feeling between us, so here's what I suggest. You buy my secret set-up from me for £150,000, which fairly reflects the value of the plant. I, in turn, reimburse you the £75,000 you're out of pocket. You provide your own staff to run the whole business from production to distribution. I will give whatever training is needed and then bow out completely. Now, how does that sound?"

"A little bird told me that a certain well known insurance company paid for your equipment, Harry. I don't think it would be morally right for me to reset stolen goods. No! Here's what we'll do. You can retire, I'll relieve you of the responsibility for the whole operation and, as a goodwill gesture, I'll write off my £75,000 loss. Now, I can't say fairer than that, can I?"

A total take over, with no compensation at all! Harry had in fact expected no better terms and was relieved that he was being offered immediate redundancy. There was no way he wanted to be in thrall to Tennant. Nothing had been said about his two printers up in Scotland. Harry quickly decided to leave it at that. If David and Brian wanted to work for Tennant, that was their business. Meanwhile, as Tennant did not seem to know of their existence, Harry decided to say nothing.

"I'm far from happy with that, Mr Tennant," said Harry. "You can make over a million a week if you get decent staff. I've only been playing at the game and have never got near realising the full potential of the equipment. With your contacts, you could set up a round-the-clock operation and really clean up. I think £75,000 is a very reasonable price."

"Harry," the fat man said slowly. "Harry, I don't think you can be listening. I'm not here to haggle. I'm telling you what's what and you're being slow on the uptake. Shall I ask my minders to step in and explain my terms to you in their own inimitable style? I find that most people understand them very quickly, even when they have failed to understand me at my most straightforward."

"I understand," said Harry, quickly. "All I ask is give me

until the weekend to wind up and clear out and then it's all yours. Is that fair?"

"I'm a reasonable man, as you know," replied Tennant. "Now, no clever stuff. You can take whatever printed stock you have at this point in time. I'll get four of my boys to stay with you to help you between now and Saturday, just in case you get any bright ideas meanwhile. Now exactly where is the plant?"

"Scotland, hidden away in the remote Highlands," replied Harry.

"Altnariach, I presume?"

That really shook Harry. Tennant seemed to know everything. Was there nowhere unreached by the loathsome man's tentacles?

"I suggest we drive up on Saturday," said Harry, trying to hide his surprise. "There's no need to leave your heavies here with me. I'm not going to slip up to Scotland this side of the weekend and having them hanging around here will just attract attention. None of the Smither's staff have any inkling about the Highland set-up and it would be silly at this stage to give them any suspicions. I've every bit as much to lose as you so I'm not going to try any funny stuff."

"Just the same, I am a cautious man and you're very valuable to me at the minute. I wouldn't like anything to happen to you, so I'll arrange round-the-clock protection for you. Don't worry! It will be very discreet. You may not even notice it yourself, but it will be in place. Now, I must be off. I've things to do, printing staff to recruit, paper to organise and so on. I'm sure you understand all the problems we printing firm proprietors have to grapple with! I'll be back in touch before the week-end. Bye, Harry. It's been nice doing business with you!"

Harry was both furious and frustrated. For once he regretted his own obsession with security. There was no way to communicate with David and Brian without one of Tennant's minders finding out. The bulk of the stock of money was now safely in Carlisle, not at the transport depot but in a large lock-up garage whose existence was known only to David and himself. However, he had wanted to give Brian and David the chance to slip away without ever meeting Tennant. Now that would be impossible. He greatly regretted this. Harry had his own moral standards and he played strictly fairly with his confederates. All the genuine money accumulated as a result of the sale of the counterfeit stuff had been scrupulously divided on a pre-arranged basis: 50% to Harry and 25% each to Brian and David and each had his share banked away, so slipping off was a realistic option. However, it was too risky to try to get a message to them so they would just have to take their chances with the new management.

Chapter 24

Kathleen knew her discovery of the charred piece of paper was potentially very important. The next day she scribbled a note to her boss and sent it with the scrap by post, Recorded Delivery. She also tried to phone, but he was not available and, rather than talk to anyone else, she said she would ring back. It was mid-morning when Kathleen and Dougal arrived back at the marshes. They had kitted themselves out with binoculars and cameras in an effort to tone in with the ornithologists who were the usual visitors to this quiet and out of the way spot. They could hardly risk doing a blatant house-to-house search, so they worked their way northwards down the Spey valley, unobtrusively snooping at all the cottages, farms and houses as they went. It was hardly a comprehensive search. However, there were some groups of buildings which so obviously had several different inhabitants that it seemed unlikely that some clandestine printing press could be concealed in them without an unbelievably large and varied group of people being involved. Likewise, there were several small cottages which the two thought could be safely eliminated because they were just too small to conceal a fair size industrial operation.

Kathleen fancied one particular farm as the best bet. It was isolated. An attempt at conversation with a surly character who happened to be at the gate as they passed was rebuffed with a rudeness which was uncharacteristic of this part of the world. There was a bonfire burning at the far end of the yard and it was quite conceivable that embers from it could blow into the bird sanctuary. Dougal felt the hypocrisy of his position acutely, but at the same time realised that he could only tell what he knew at this stage at the cost of revealing how he had been playing Kathleen along. The two lingered in the vicinity, taking great interest in the activities of a handy red-kite which was swooping to and fro. More than an hour of the afternoon was taken up with trying to keep this particular farm under observation when the school bus rolled up and stopped outside. A total of five children of varying ages streamed off it and entered the gate. They were greeted by the surly fellow in a way which revealed that he was their father and that this was him in his most cheerful and welcoming mood. With reluctance, Kathleen agreed she had got it wrong. It would be impossible to run a secret printing operation with a clutch of kids like that around.

They called off their search in late afternoon, Kathleen depressed at finding no positive leads, Dougal making a good job of looking equally downcast. He managed to persuade her that they had done well in that they had eliminated at least two thirds of the likely premises and he reminded her that tomorrow was another day.

Chapter 25

The next day was Saturday, a day of action for all the major players in the forgery business.

Jimmy Tennant called round at Harry's house at 9am in the Rolls. His driver and one of the minders sat in the front, whilst Harry sat beside Tennant in the back. A Jaguar carrying another four burly characters followed the Rolls up the M1. There was not much to say, so Harry gazed despondently out of the window for most of the journey.

David and Brian were feeling frustrated. They had, as arranged with Harry, finished printing every last sheet of paper and David had transported the goods to Carlisle. The last two days had been spent cooling their heels as they waited for Harry. They had expected him before now and felt confident he would at least make contact, if not come, that week-end.

Dougal and Kathleen made a leisurely start to the day. Kathleen again phoned her boss. As it was Saturday, she was not greatly surprised that he was not expected in until later that morning. She would ring again from Kingussie.

Chief Superintendent Stanley Morton, who was both Kathleen's boss and the officer heading the special forgery team, arrived about 10.30am. He opened Kathleen's letter and examined with growing excitement the enclosure. The next fifteen minutes were spent on the telephone issuing instructions here and there.

His assistant hurriedly assembled as many of the team as

could be mustered in the short time available.

"We've a major breakthrough!" Morton almost shouted in a rare display of excitement. "That girl's stumbled on the clue we've been looking for. We'll fly to Inverness at once. Get that organised, Ronnie."

Ronnie nodded and slipped out of the room. "Peter, will you contact the Chief and get him to smooth the way for us with the Highland Constabulary." Peter left the room.

"Ken, you get hold of that fellow Flint, will you. He's done a lot of the ground work and I wouldn't like him to be left out."

At this point a telephonist stuck his head round the door. "Excuse me, sir. That's Kathleen on the phone now. A call-box in some unpronounceable part of Scotland. Shall I put it through?"

"Of course, man, and be quick about it," replied the impatient Morton. He picked up the phone on his desk. A pin-drop silence filled the room as all tried to hear both sides of the conversation. They were out of luck. What they did hear was: "Hullo! Hullo! Kathleen? Hullo! Yes, it's me. Looks as though you've come up with the goods this time. Jolly good work.......What? You'll do no such thing!.....No! I positively forbid it!..... No! You listen to me. You wait there until the whole squad's assembled....... What do you mean, you can't do any harm making a few preliminary enquiries? You don't know what you may be getting into. ....No, we can't get everything ready before nightfall. We'll go in at first light..... What do you mean, we don't know where to go?..... No! You're not to go snooping around!... Oh, blast those pips. Put some more money in, girl! What do you mean, you're out of change? Hullo! Hullo! Oh, blast! She's gone. I'm sure the headstrong woman did that deliberately. Higgins! Higgins, trace that call. Not that it'll do us any good if it's a call-box. The stupid woman's off on a single-handed hunt for the forgers."

Before resuming their search, Dougal and Kathleen stopped in Aviemore and spent an hour separately, going from shop to shop, making the odd trivial purchase whilst trying to engage the assistants in conversation about the various properties around the marshes. This proved fruitless. Very few seemed to have any real local knowledge. For the first time, Dougal noticed that you were more likely to be served by someone with an English accent than someone with a Scottish one.

When he commented on this to Kathleen, she replied, "That's because the Scots are all down south where the best jobs are! You've no idea how often you hear Scottish accents in England, especially in London. I don't know where the English police force would be without the Scots, particularly the Met.! Never mind that, did you get anything useful?"

"No, not really. The most helpful was the estate agency. I told him we were hoping to buy a holiday home near the bird sanctuary. He looked gloomy and said he knew of nothing. I said we wanted something remote. That only seemed to make it worse. However, I've got the names of three places which might fit the bill, but are all not for sale. We might as well start there."

The first was so remote that the rest of the morning was spent trying to find it. When they did, they discovered it was let, occupied by a Buddhist group who used it as a retreat. The caretaker was very friendly when they enquired about property to let or for sale, but assured them there was no immediate prospect of the retreat being for sale. He did, however, point out a spot on the map where he said there was a burnt-out ruin which, he believed, still had usable stables and cottages in the grounds.

As it was early afternoon, they decided to go on into Kingussie for lunch and to resume their investigation later. It was therefore past 3pm when they arrived at the top of a steep, overgrown driveway which led down to buildings which were nearly completely screened by the trees a couple of hundred yards away. At the top of the drive was a gardener's lodge which looked so run-down it was hard to guess whether it was inhabited or not. Kathleen drove past without significantly slowing up.

As they passed, Dougal pointed out the battered sign-post, 'Altnariach.' "That looks interesting," he said. "Well, what do you think?"

"By far the most promising so far. What's the next move?"

"What we ought to do is to wait for the police. Look, let's find somewhere to hide the car and I'll go back on foot for a snoop. If I'm not back within, say, forty minutes, you call out the cavalry."

"Oh no you don't! I'm not cooling my heels here while you have all the fun. I'm going. You can stay here."

They argued on until they came to the inevitable compromise. They both would go. A hundred yards or so from the driveway, they had noticed a field with its gate open. If they drove the car in it would be screened from the road by a dense hedge. A couple of miles up the road, they found a wide enough spot to turn the car in and they returned, turning confidently into the gate. The entry to the field was very rough and the car took a battering as they bounced their way in. However, it was now safely out of sight. They quietly left the vehicle and let fifteen minutes or so go by to see if anyone would investigate their arrival. In that time, nothing stirred. No vehicles used the road and not a sound came from the buildings below them.

The gatehouse was every bit as dilapidated as they had thought, but a whisker of smoke from the chimney told them that, in spite of appearances, it was inhabited, whether or not the occupant was at home at the present moment. Keeping to the grass verge, they noiselessly slipped past the house and down the drive. At the foot stood the burnt out shell of what had once been a piece of Victorian magnificence. The splendid porch was still intact, though heavily screened by ivy. The massive door seemed to have escaped the fire, only to fall victim to years of neglect. It hung sadly on its rusted hinges and looked as if any attempt to move it would lead to its final disintegration. Beyond, were the gaunt walls of the house, with mature trees growing up within it to heights exceeding that of the gables. The subtle smell of rot and decay lingered in the still air.

A slight noise on the gravel beyond the house alerted them to someone's approach. Dougal drew Kathleen into the shadow of the overgrown porch. An ancient figure staggered past. Staggered was the appropriate word! Even at ten yards range, Dougal was sure he could smell the drink. They waited until, at last, the old man had weaved his way up to the gatehouse and they heard the door slam shut.

"Not my image of a criminal mastermind, but you never know," grinned Kathleen. "Let's see what's round the back."

Cautiously, the two passed the ruined mansion and found themselves faced with a high, castellated wall with a large double door set in it. Dougal sidled up to the door. There were no handy cracks to look through. He stood still and listened. There was absolute silence. Very carefully, he turned the handle. The door was firmly locked. He signalled to Kathleen and they moved on past the stable block. Behind the ground fell away sharply. There were no windows in the wall at all. Any windows giving light to the buildings must face on to the courtyard which was obviously behind the locked double doors. A hundred yards farther down the track were gardens which were so heavily overgrown that it was hard to realise they had ever been there. The crumbling walls of more buildings were beyond, again heavily shrouded in ivy. Silently they approached. The door of a potting shed was open and they looked in. To their surprise, it was clearly still in use, not as a potting shed, but as a pottery. There were two electric ovens and a potter's wheel. On shelves round the walls were ornamental pots in various stages of completion.

"I think we're barking up the wrong tree once again," muttered Kathleen. "It's either very ingenious cover or we're away off course."

They were standing just inside the shed when a noise from where they had come attracted their attention. The door of the courtyard opened and a red-headed youth carrying a shotgun emerged. He closed the door, went off round the front of the ruin and disappeared into the wood.

"I'm sure he didn't lock that door! Dougal breathed. "Let's have a quick snoop. If there's nothing suspicious we might as well give up."

They hurried back up to the doorway. As they approached it they heard a distant shot, then, a few seconds later, a second one. Dougal tried the door and it swung open. Ahead lay a long courtyard, empty except for a rather tired looking Land Rover at the far end. Half way along was an open door. Both of them crept up to it. In the surprisingly bright, fluorescently lit interior, a man was tidying up what was obviously a well-equipped printing workshop.

"Bingo!" Kathleen breathed with a broad grin. "Now let's get out while the going's good!"

As quietly as they had come, they made their way back to the doorway. Just as they were stepping through it, the red-haired youth stepped in. It would be hard to say who got the greater surprise. Dougal's mind raced. How do you talk your way out of this one? He didn't get a chance. The lad dropped the two ducks he was holding and levelled his shotgun.

"Back inside," he growled. For the second time that summer, Dougal found himself faced with the two eyes of a twin-barrelled shotgun. Somehow, this time he was even more worried.

The kid was obviously much more scared than they were and the idea of a frightened man waving a shotgun at point-blank range was at least mildly disconcerting. He raised his hands slowly and stepped backwards into the courtyard, at the same time trying to put himself between Kathleen and the muzzle which was only three foot from them.

"In there!" Commanded the youth, gesturing with the gun to a very high door on the right. The door was secured with a massive hasp and staple, through which was a heavy spike. Dougal pulled out the spike. For a fleeting second he wondered if he could use it on the man, but the other read his mind.

"Lay it down real slow," he said pointing the gun at Dougal's midriff. "Now, get inside. Any trouble and the lady gets it first."

There was no point in arguing and, submissively, the two walked in. The door was slammed shut. The darkness was intense after the bright sunshine, but a little light did penetrate through an extremely dirty, heavily barred window. There was a strange noise outside which neither could identify. It was only Brian being sick. Then they heard the rumble of a heavy engine. Peering through the dirty window, Dougal saw the youth manoeuvre the Land Rover so that its back was hard up against the door, clearly a man who took no chances.

Inspecting his new prison took Dougal even less time than that at Kinloch Esk. No handy bits of wood. No scissor jacks. Only one empty five-gallon oil drum, a few short coils of fencing wire, a rotten wheel-barrow and a lot of dirty straw on the floor and that was about it. The coach-house was about twenty feet square with solid stone walls, a stone-flagged floor and a very high plastered ceiling. The door and the window were quickly examined and abandoned as hopeless.

Whilst he was doing his inspection, a sudden thought struck Dougal. That kid was scared nearly witless, yet he had the upper hand, or, more precisely, his hand held the gun. But was the gun loaded? He had shot his two ducks and was returning. Would he have bothered reloading? Small wonder the youngster was so worried! There was no point in crying over spilt milk. He decided not to pass these thoughts on to Kathleen.

"I'm sorry, but I seem to have really landed you in it this time," he said apologetically.

"No! It was me that got you into this mess. I didn't tell you, but my boss told me in no uncertain terms not to do anything until he came. But I was too pig-headed to listen! I'm sorry I let my enthusiasm run away with me. It's difficult to see how they can let us live. We know too much. And let's face it, they'll go down for at least as long for forgery as they will for murder. They've nothing to lose."

Realistic, but not exactly cheering, thought Dougal. Kathleen went on. "There's something else I want to tell you, in case I don't get a chance later. I think I'm falling in love with you, Dougal."

A fine time to discover that, Dougal thought but did not say.

What he did say was, "I'll ask you to repeat that when we're safely out of here. Now, do you see that damp patch up there?"

He pointed up through the gloom to a large dark patch in the ceiling. It spread out from the outside wall for about six feet roughly halfway between the front and the back.

"If you get on my shoulders and use my stick, you might just manage to hack a hole through the plaster. With any luck, the lathe behind it will be rotten. The building's single storey, so there will be no floor above. I don't know how you get out of the roof space but this must be a step in the right direction."

He lent his back against the wall and cupped his hands in front of him. Kathleen gripped the handle of his walking-stick in her teeth and swiftly shinned up to stand a little unsteadily on his shoulders. Suddenly, he was delighted that she was so slimly built. Balancing precariously, she attacked the plaster above her with the walking-stick. Soon great lumps of rotten plaster were thudding down round about them.

His eyes tight shut to keep the dust and muck out of them, Dougal's thoughts went back over the unexpected events of the last few weeks. He remembered grappling with the question "To be, or

142

not to be?" and suddenly he knew his answer. To die or to live? He now desperately wanted to live! If Kathleen and he could only get out of this prison, there was undoubtedly a future for them together!

When she had exposed an area of about two foot square of the lathe, Kathleen reversed the walking-stick and hooked the handle over the thin, rotten wood. It tore like paper. In minutes she had a hole big enough to climb through. She reached through and groped for the rafters on either side. Then she gingerly stood on Dougal's head with one foot. He reached up and eased his hand under the other.

"One, two three and heave!" he said as he boosted her upwards. Using all her strength, she pulled herself up into the dark void above.

"Right! I'm up! Now what?" she called down.

"What's it like up there?" Dougal asked in a stage whisper.

"Even darker than down there. There's a skylight about twenty feet along. We might get out there but how are you going to get up?"

"Easy! We'll make a ladder! Look, I'll feed up a piece of wire. You catch it. Then we'll use it to hoist up some more. There must be roof ties or something you can tie it on to. Pass down a loop and I'll form a foothold about four feet up. I can use the oil-drum for the first step. Then a second strand will give me a foothold at the six foot mark and a third at the eight. Got the idea?"

"You're a genius! Anyone would think you'd had lots of experience of being locked up by angry men with shotguns! Pass up the wire!"

It was one of those rare jobs which proved easier than either of them had expected. In less than twenty minutes, Dougal joined Kathleen in the roof void and had pulled the makeshift ladder up after him. In another couple of minutes, they had forced open the skylight. Now came the time for a difficult decision. Should they risk venturing out in daylight, knowing they would be sitting ducks if they were spotted? Or should they risk waiting for an hour as the sun sank over the western hills?

Had they heard the conversations that had taken place in the press-room, they need not have worried.

"You what?" exclaimed David. "You left the door unlocked! How could you be so stupid! Now what are we going to do? If Jimmy Tennant turns up, he won't hesitate. Those two will be history. But he's going to be hopping mad at us! And if we let them go? They'll have the cops here within the hour. Not only will we be banged up, but Tennant will find out at the trial. We'll never live to finish our sentences!"

"I'm sorry, but if you had had the sense to keep the press-room door shut, they would have seen nothing. It's just as much your fault as mine. I'm not getting involved in murder! I'm getting out before Tennant gets here."

"And do you think you can hide from Jimmy Tennant for ever? Look! We're in a mess, but let's not fall out or panic. We'll wait until its dark and then we'll scarper. If Tennant turns up before that, I suppose we'll have to tell him, but the chances are he won't. Now let's load up the van. We can hide it up the back drive where it will be out of sight of both the house and the road."

The activity in the courtyard of these preparations for departure puzzled the two in the roof-space, but also made decision-making easy. They would have to wait for darkness. The suspense was hard to bear. They watched the red-headed lad drive the van out of one of the coach-houses, load it up and drive off through the double doors. Shortly after, he returned on foot, carefully locking the doors. He paused to make sure that their late prison was still securely locked, then disappeared into the building. The sun had now set and the courtyard below was a pool of darkness, lit only where shafts of light streamed from such rooms as had lights on.

"I think we make a move now," muttered Dougal, easing himself out through the skylight. The roof was slippery, but by pressing his foot in the skylight aperture, he was able to reach the ridge above and to haul himself up. Kathleen soon followed. They balanced on the ridge.

"Now what?" She whispered.

"Ideally, we drop down on the outside. It's awfully high, though and the ground below is desperately uneven. It's just asking for a broken leg or worse. It wouldn't be so bad if you could see the ground, but it's now so dark."

"Well, you can't have it both ways. At least we've got the cover of darkness."

As this whispered conversation was proceeding, headlights of two cars streamed down the steep drive. Hope surged in Kathleen's heart. "The cavalry!" she muttered in Dougal's ear. The cars swung round to line up on the doors and, as they did so, the headlights of the second illuminated the first.

"Unless your boss drives a Rolls Royce, I think it's more bandits." Dougal whispered. "We'd better get off this ridge in case they can see us against the sky."

The far side of the roof was thickly coated with a slimy green moss. With difficulty, they trailed their legs over the ridge and hung on, knowing that if they lost their grip, they would start on an unstoppable slide down the roof and be launched into the black depths below. The red-headed youth came out and opened the door. The Rolls swept in, closely followed by a purring Jaguar. Both cars were then parked alongside the Land Rover. Four men alighted from each vehicle. There was a buzz of conversation which the watchers on the roof could not make out. Then all the men went into the press-room, closing the door after them.

"I don't think we dare delay any longer," said Dougal. "It

looks as though the boss-man has arrived and they will probably decide very quickly what to do with us. I think our best bet it is to drop on to the canvas roof of the Land Rover and then hope we can open the doors. We may not have much time. You go first as you're a lot lighter than me. I don't want you stranded up here if the canvas doesn't take my weight."

They pulled themselves up on to the ridge and worked their way along it until they were above the Land Rover. At this point, Kathleen caught sight of a bright light slightly above them to the south-east. For a moment she was baffled. Then she said, "The moon! The harvest moon!" Sure enough, in a matter of only a minute or so a gigantic full moon appeared above the horizon, exposing them to anyone who happened to look up.

"Quick, Kathleen! Jump! Then hide between the cars. I'll be right behind you."

Kathleen slid down the slates, caught her foot on the gutter, stood up and jumped. She landed with a soft thud on the canvas. It sagged with a slight ripping sound, but took her weight. Awkwardly, she crawled forward, slid her feet over the windscreen, stood on the bonnet and then dropped noiselessly to the ground. Dougal was just about to follow her when the press-room door opened. A man came out and strode over to the cars. Dougal held his breath. The man could not fail to see Kathleen. From his position above, Dougal could not see her, but he knew she was in the pool of darkness between the cars. The man walked right up to where Dougal was sure Kathleen was. What happened next, he could not make out. He glimpsed Kathleen's blond hair as she stood up in front of the man. There was a muffled thud and the man's body sagged and fell to the ground. Then there was only silence. Dougal wasted no more time. He slid down the slates and launched himself on to the canvas below. This time, it did tear, but it broke his fall. A few seconds later he was crouched beside

Kathleen alongside the prostate figure.

"Whatever did you do?" He asked in amazement.

"A little trick John taught me. He worried about me being alone while he was posted abroad, so he taught me how to look after myself, not that I've ever needed it before. Quick! help me tuck him out of sight. He'll wake up in a few hours with an awfully sore neck, but otherwise none the worse."

Chapter 26

In the press-room, Tennant had completed his preliminary inspection. He was visibly impressed. Meanwhile two of his henchmen who were obviously printers, were being taken through the complexities of the numbering process by David. Brian was hovering in the back-ground, getting more and more nervous. At last, he felt that the time had come to tell, first Harry, then Tennant about the captives. A dreadful hush followed.

"We'll just have to get rid of them," declared Tennant firmly. "Bruce and Nicky, you see to tit."

"Now, wait a minute, Mr Tennant," said David. "I want nothing to do with this. I don't mind forgery, but I draw a line at murder. I want out and I want out now!"

"OK! OK! I understand. If you want out, you can get out. Bruce! Nicky! See these two off, will you."

Brian led the way out of the press-room, closely followed by David and the two minders. As they stepped out into the moonlit courtyard, Bruce drew out a revolver and shot David in the back. David dropped to his knees muttering, "He who must sup with the devil, must use a long spoon." He coughed up blood, fell forward and died.

The revolver swung round to Brian, but he had had just a split second's warning. The gun fired just as he ducked and the bullet slammed harmlessly into a door on the far side of the courtyard. Brian dashed through the door of one of the stables and

148

slammed it shut. He had barely thrust home the big bolts when a heavy shoulder thudded against it.

Quickly, he shinned up a vertical ladder to the hayloft above. In his wildest nightmares, Brian had never dreamt of this kind of scenario. He had, however, often thought of his tactics if the place were ever raided by the police. On the face of it, the place was a natural trap as all the doors of the buildings opened on to the courtyard and it in turn had only one gateway. However, from the haylofts on both sides, Brian had made his own emergency exits. Both had windows in the gables which looked out over the deep ditch far below and the marshes beyond. From both windows, Brian had strung a length of fencewire, anchoring one end firmly to one of the roof-ties in the hayloft and the other to a Scots pine nearly 300 yards on top of a small scrub covered knoll beyond the ditch. A pulley and a short length of heavy rope completed this aerial runway. With a metallic whine, he shot off into the darkness, leaving his pursuers to find an empty stable.

Harry nearly fainted at the two gunshots. He turned aghast to Tennant. The man was his usual unflappable self.

"They wanted out. Bruce and Nicky have taken them out. End of problem. We'll get rid of the bodies along with those two busybodies."

He walked out. Harry, feeling he had no option and acutely conscious of the fact that he had four of Tennant's thugs behind him, followed. Outside, they found that Bruce and Nicky had kicked in the door and discovered Brian's secret railway to freedom.

"After him!" Tennant roared. "Ron! Mike! Fred! You go with Nicky and get him. There are torches in the Jag. Spread out and round him up. You'll be able to trap him between here and the river if you get a move on. Bruce! You and Tom come with me. You, too, Harry! Where's Benny? Anyone seen Benny? He went out for my brief-case. Where the devil's the fool got to? Don't hang around. You know what needs doing! Get on with it!"

Dougal and Kathleen, crouched between the Rolls and the Jaguar, had witnessed all this with horror. So far, they had avoided detection, but as the four men started in their direction, their luck seemed to be running out.

"Wait a minute," said Tennant, pausing. "Harry, you reverse the Land Rover back there. Tom. You help him dump that body in it, then drive back here. Bruce'll have the other two ready for loading when you get back."

Harry felt his head whirl. He swayed, leant on the wing of the Jaguar and was violently sick. Tennant gave a deep sigh. "I'm afraid you're not up to playing big boy's games, Harry. I'm sorry."

He nodded to Bruce who promptly shot Harry through the heart. He slid down the bonnet of the Jaguar and collapsed in a heap in front of it.

"Right, load him on too. Pick up that other guy then we'll chuck the other two on top. We won't wait for them to bring back that red-haired idiot. We can dispose of him later."

Tennant strode on past the two cars without spotting Kathleen and Dougal in the shadows. The man called Tom jumped into the Land Rover and it roared into life. He swung it forward and round to face the gate. Then he reversed back to where David's body lay. Leaving the engine running he went round the back and dropped the tailgate. He was a big man, but still he struggled to load the inert form single-handed. He had just done this when there was a shout from Tennant. He dashed back to where he found Tennant and Bruce shining their torches round the empty coach house. As the man ran passed the two cars, Dougal nudged Kathleen's arm. He nodded to the Land Rover and the two sprinted across the yard and scrambled into it.

"Get down as low as you can. We're going through the

doors."

Dougal engaged the four wheel-drive, thrust the gear-stick into first, revved the engine to a scream and let out the clutch. The heavy vehicle lurched forward. He slammed it into second gear. A fusillade of shots rang out and he heard the bullets rip through the canvas. He crouched as low as he could in his seat and charged at the huge doors. With a thunder-clap, they burst open. He yanked the wheel round and started up the drive. There was now a howl from the engine. Dougal guessed that the radiator had been forced back on to the cooling fan. The water would be pouring out and the vehicle would soon seize up. No matter! The Escort was waiting. Kathleen slid up in her seat. Both headlights were smashed, but the moon shone in shafts through the trees sufficiently for Dougal to steer a straight enough course up the pot-holed drive. He stopped at the road.

"You get the Escort. This thing's nearly done for. I'll block the drive with it."

Kathleen jumped down and sprinted along to where they had parked the Escort. She jumped in. It started at the first swing on the starter. Quickly she reversed out and drove along to the head of the drive. Meanwhile, Dougal had done a three-point turn and the Land Rover was now pointing back down the drive. At that moment the Rolls surged out of the shattered doors below and its headlights lit up the whole drive. Without hesitation, Dougal revved up and roared down the drive. He slipped the gear into neutral and leapt from the moving vehicle, performing a shoulder roll that his para instructors would have been proud of. The Land Rover lumbered on down the track, accelerating on the downward gradient. The driver of the Rolls realised too late that the on-coming vehicle was driverless. He slammed his foot on the brakes and swerved, but there was nowhere to go on the narrow tree-lined drive. The lordly radiator of the Rolls crumpled as two tons of uncontrolled Land Rover slammed into it.

A Rolls Royce is built with the safety of its VIP occupants very much in mind, so it was no surprise that Tennant and his two henchmen were shaken but unharmed. Swearing fluently, Bruce staggered out and blazed away at Dougal's fleeing form. The bullets whistled dangerously close but, unharmed, he scrambled into the waiting Escort.

"Go! Go! Go!" He shouted, and the car shot forward.

"I hate to say this," said Kathleen. "One of our front tyres is flat. It must have been that dreadful gateway into the field. I don't know how far we'll get."

"Only a few hundred yards, I imagine. If only it had been a rear one! Take it easy and we'll see how far we can go. It'll be several minutes before they can clear the drive and come after us."

Chapter 27

At the police headquarters in Inverness, the evening was taken up with preparations for a major operation at first light the following morning, about 4.30am. Several rural bobbies who would regard themselves as having an exciting day if half a dozen sheep strayed on to the main Perth-Inverness road, found themselves ordered to Inverness and thrust into the company of very senior officers, both from the Highland force and from London. Together, they pored over maps, pooling their considerable local knowledge and eventually narrowing the possible locations for the secret press down to three.

Chief Superintendent Morton personally visited Kathleen's aunt. It was 10.30pm and there was no word from her and her male companion. Mrs Dryden was unworried, at least until he arrived.

"They're old enough to look after themselves without me fussing over them," she said. "Sooner or later, they'll discover they are in love, although neither of them seems to have noticed so far. Don't you worry, sir. They'll be fine."

Morton left muttering under his breath something about sentimental rubbish, pig-headed young women and idiot men who ought not to encourage a headstrong hussy in her folly. Every thing was laid on for the morning. Two helicopters were standing by at Inverness airport and a convoy of police vehicles would muster at Aviemore at 3am. There was nothing more that he could do until then.

Chapter 28

Brian dropped to earth from his aerial run-way with a soft thud. He had often visualised having to exit in a hurry pursued by the police, but not by men with guns who shot on sight. His forward planning only went as far as getting rapidly clear of the buildings. Now he was clear, he had no coherent strategy except flight. The moon was shining brightly now and, looking back, he could see the castellated walls sharply defined against the darker background of the hills beyond. Before him and to both sides lay the trackless marshlands. He would head for the bird-sanctuary. If he could lie up somewhere there for the rest of the night, he might well be able to mingle with bird-watchers in the morning and get away unobserved. He left the shelter of the scrub. Several shots rang out from the buildings above him and he heard the thud of bullets whack into the soft ground near by. He ducked and he ran. His course was a series of involuntary zigzags as, repeatedly, he found his path blocked by a pond or a dangerous looking morass. He glanced over his shoulder. A quarter of a mile behind were the firefly-like flickers of torches. Four of them, spread out in a fan-formation. He would outrun them. Then he found himself on the banks of the River Spey. In despair he looked across the fifty yards of black, deep water. Why, oh why had he never learned to swim? He swung round to the left and started to run along the river bank. His lungs were bursting. He could not keep this up. He blundered wildly into some gorse bushes. Diving into the thickest clump he could find, he collapsed, shivering, not through cold, but through sheer, naked terror.

Back in the driveway, the three men were struggling to clear the debris of the two vehicles. The damage was surprisingly light. The Rolls was still moveable, although its nearside wing was pressing hard on the tyre. Tennant reversed it down the drive and Bruce followed, steering the free-wheeling Land Rover. Where the drive widened sufficiently, they abandoned both vehicles and raced off to the Jaguar. Pausing only to roll Harry's body clear, they leapt in and shot off up the drive.

Kathleen had driven less than half a mile when it was clear they could go no farther. Every shred of rubber was gone from the wheel and forward motion was almost non-existent as the steel rim skidded on the tarmac throwing up showers of sparks. There was an open gate on the left and Kathleen swung the car in, hoping to get it out of sight of the road. However, it stuck in the mud at the gateway and, even with Dougal pushing as hard as he could at the rear, it would go no farther.

"Shank's pony from here on," said Kathleen, scrambling out. "Let's head back parallel with the road and hope they think we would go on heading south."

"Good idea! I only hope I don't hold you up."

The two had covered less than quarter of a mile when blazing headlights could be seen flickering through the trees. A car was approaching rapidly from the direction they had come from. It might just be a motorist in a hurry, but that seemed unlikely. Kathleen and Dougal reached the cover of some patchy gorse when the car swept into view. A Jaguar! It stopped. The Jaguar! Three men leapt from it and started to search around on both sides of the road. On the far side, apart from a few birch trees immediately beside the road, there was no cover at all, only bare heather-clad hillside on which anything bigger than a football would be clearly seen in the brilliant moonlight. Once they had eliminated that, the three men held a brief conference. They then fanned out and moved steadily down the slope.

One was going to pass their hiding place too closely to miss them, so Dougal and Kathleen decided to make a run for the marshes below. Taking advantage of every last piece of scrub, they ran at a crouch. After a couple of hundred yards, a cry, followed by shots, told them they had been spotted. They ran on. The ground levelled out and became increasingly boggy underfoot. They blundered into a flock of swans who soon became very angry. Ignoring the wing-flapping and hissing they pressed on, leaving their pursuers to negotiate their way past the birds who were, by this time, exceedingly worked up. That, and a patch of cloud which briefly covered the moon, bought them valuable time. They had, at least for the timebeing, thrown off their pursuers. They lay side by side in the long reeds, struggling to get their breath back.

"Now what?" Kathleen whispered.

"I think we crawl from here on. It'll start to get light in about three hours. If we're still in the open then, I think we'll have had it. That moon's a mixed blessing. If it were totally dark, we'd be lost, but, if we're not very careful, they'll spot us by its light."

"The Spey must be about a mile away. Let's head for that. There's bound to be more cover round it's banks, and even crawling, we should be able to make it before dawn."

The next hours were a nightmare. Because they were naturally keeping to the lowest ground they could, the two were almost constantly wrist-deep in freezing water and soaked from the knees to the feet. It got worse.

They were resting under a scrubby gorse bush, when a dry cough close by warned them of the approach of one of the gunmen. Through the gloom, they could just make out his form, picking his way through the marsh towards them. They froze. Nearer and nearer he came, until they could hear the mud squelching under his feet. Kathleen nodded to Dougal and the two slithered down into the peaty brown waters of a pool. There they wriggled until their bodies were submerged in the mud at the bottom of the shallow pond. The footsteps came ever closer. They could sense, rather than see, the figure standing above them. He flashed his torch out across the water. Both the fugitives took a deep breath and pressed their faces down into the muddy bottom of the pool. When they could stay submerged no longer, they cautiously lifted their heads. By then the torch beam had moved to the right and, with indescribable relief, they heard the sloshing footsteps move away. After several more minutes immersed in the icy water, they pulled themselves on to the relatively drier ground by the gorse bush. The gunman was only fifty yards away, standing motionless, obviously waiting for the slightest sound or movement that would guide him to his prey. Then from farther south came a splash in the reeds. The man dashed in that direction, only to encounter another swan. His furious curses echoed back to where the shivering pair silently lay. However, he was now far enough away for them to move forward safely.

The sky was lightening in the east when they reached the banks of the river. They had lost sight of their pursuers completely, keeping as they did, to the low-lying ground. At the river bank, they lay flat and, raising their heads, looked cautiously around. Upstream, half a mile away, was a man on the bank. Likewise, downstream, a little farther away, was a second, but a mere two hundred yards away, standing on a small knoll and searching all around him, was the man they called Bruce.

Chapter 29

It was 3am in Aviemore. The holiday village was asleep. The traffic through the town was negligible and that on the bypass too distant to disturb the dreamy peace. The only place awake was the police station. Police cars and mini-buses spilt over from its over-crowded car-park into the public one next door. An air of expectancy hung over the place. Local officers were quietly betting with one another on the winner of the three chosen locations for the hidden press. Everyone was wound up waiting for the word to go. When at last it did come, the vehicles moved out, each with instructions to take up positions and await orders. By 4am, in a dozen or more country lanes, police vehicles crammed with tense officers, were in place. As the first rays of thin morning sunshine lit up the highest tops on the west side of the broad Spey valley, the order to move in came. At one lonely farm and at an isolated shooting lodge, the startled, innocent occupants found their buildings surrounded as police officers hammered on their doors.

Two police Land Rovers, followed by a minibus packed with policemen swept down the drive to the burnt-out shell of the Altnariach shooting lodge. Six officers surrounded the Rolls and the Land Rover. A cursory inspection revealed the dead David in the back of the latter. A series of radio messages followed and all the other units began to close in. Another body was found in the yard along with a surviving casualty. The buildings were rapidly searched and found to be deserted.

Morton stood on the stairhead overlooking the marshes.

"Scramble the choppers!" He barked. "I want every inch of those marshes swept. So far we've only found men. If they've touched that girl, heaven help them!"

He climbed down the steps.

"Have we got roadblocks on every possible road? Good!"

The other vehicles were streaming in. One which had come up from the south reported difficulty in passing a deserted Jaguar half a mile down the road. Morton commandeered the Land Rover nearest the gate and shot off up the drive. In minutes he was walking round the Jaguar. In the field by the road was a rather sad-looking Escort with virtually no front wheel. It was quite clear what had happened. Morton radioed for all available personnel to sweep the marshes, then started off down through the field to see what he could find in the daylight that was strengthening moment by moment.

Chapter 30

Brian lay prostrate in a bog. Behind him was the river, an uncrossable barrier. He raised his head slowly. The nearest of Tennant's minders was only a hundred yards away. The other three were twice that distance, but the gap was closing. As long as it was dark, he had been able to hide, but the sun was now rising. He lay in the water, chilled to the marrow and shivering convulsively. An alien noise, like an angry bee, came to his ear. It grew in intensity. Then he recognised the distinctive throb of a helicopter's rotors. He rolled on his side and looked up. It broke his limited horizon. It was followed by a second. The first did a low sweep overhead. The second dipped out of sight. He wriggled forward to a position where he could see the ground ahead more clearly. A figure in blue wearing a baseball cap and wielding a rifle appeared momentarily on a hummock just beyond the nearest of Tennant's men. Then there was a second and a third. The first raised something which to Brian's reeling brain looked like a bazooka. As a deafening voice roared out, he realised it was a loudhailer.

"Armed police! Lay down your weapons! Step backwards very slowly! Raise your hands high above your heads! You! The one lying flat in the grass! That means you!"

Brian looked round. Tennant's men were all standing with their hands held high. Very slowly, quaking like a leaf, Brian rose to his knees with his hands above his head. With legs like jelly, he staggered to his feet. Never was a man so glad to be arrested.

To Die or to Live?

Chapter 31

Two miles south, Dougal and Kathleen had watched with real trepidation as the first rays of dawn twinkled across the sky . They were hidden on the river bank but it was now obvious that Bruce reckoned time was on his side and that there would be no hiding place for the fugitives in daylight.

"We could swim across the river, but we'll stick out a mile as we get out on the far bank," Dougal whispered. "Our only hope would be if we can make it to that clump of gorse the other side. I votes we stay put unless he moves nearer. If he comes, we'll try swimming. If we're spotted, we dive, turn right and surface back on this side farther down-stream."

Kathleen nodded her agreement. The daylight strengthened. It was then that Bruce started to move slowly towards them. Wordlessly they communicated with each other and slipped into the river. Just when Kathleen was beginning to hope they might make it, a shot rang out and there was a splash only inches from her head. She gulped a lungfull of air and duck-dived, colliding with Dougal as, together, they both turned under water. In a slow strong breast-stroke, she propelled herself rapidly down the river, swinging in towards the bank when she could hold her breath no longer. Dougal surfaced a moment later a yard or two downstream. Nodding to a thick clump of reeds, he motioned to her to take cover. He wriggled up the bank and peered out through the dense grass at the top.

Bruce was only fifty yards away, but making heavy weather of struggling through a bog. He looked up, caught sight of Dougal and fired. The slug whistled past Dougal's left ear. Bruce swore and plunged farther into the bog. Suddenly he was up to his waist. Dougal raised his head and another bullet whistled by. He slithered back and worked his way downstream a little, reckoning that if he showed himself again, he could draw the gunman away from Kathleen. He peered over the bank again. Bruce was now chest deep and needing help. Dougal shouted to him and got another bullet whistling past his head by way of reply. He flung himself flat. There was a pause. He looked up carefully again, just in time to see an arm, the hand still clutching the revolver, waving out of the bog. Then that, too, was sucked under. The mire closed in as though there had never been a man disturbing it at all.

Dougal rose to his knees in a state of shock. The other two had heard the gunfire and were closing in. He slipped back to where Kathleen was half in, half out of the river.

"The immediate danger's past, but the other two thugs are closing in. Are you game for another swim?"

Mutely, she nodded and the two slipped quietly back into the river. This time they made it safely to the far shore. They pulled their now numb bodies out and had just reached the cover of a gnarled willow when several shots rang out and bullets whistled past or smashed into the tree. They lay prostrate behind the limited protection it offered. The two men were closing in on the far bank. With a sense of helplessness, Dougal realised that the tree was too slender to provide cover for both of them if their enemies strung themselves out along the riverside. Certainly, lying flat where they were, they made a very difficult target, but it seemed inevitable that sooner or later a good shot would get them. Alternatively, one gun-man could pin them down, while the other found a crossing point and out-flanked them. He looked behind him. Nearly a hundred yards of hopelessly exposed ground to the nearest reasonable cover. Clearly, Kathleen and he had used up their share of good luck.

"I'm so sorry I dragged you into this mess," he murmured.

Before she could reply, a new sound shattered the peace. A helicopter swept up the river and a loudhailer was ordering Tennant and his crony to drop their guns. Dougal grabbed Kathleen's hand and clasped her to him. Then, together they rose to their knees. In the growing daylight, they could see blue-clad figures closing in on the men on the far bank from three separate directions. The two men now stood motionless, one upstream of them, one downstream, both with their hands in the air.

"The cavalry," gasped Kathleen. "A bit behind schedule, but just in the nick of time!"

She was shivering convulsively and Dougal wrapped his arms round her.

"I think there was something you were going to say to me again once we got safely out of that prison," he said.

Chapter 32

A helicopter swept Dougal and Kathleen to the Duke of Gordon Hotel in Kingussie where the manager and staff treated the shivering pair like royalty. Later, well-showered, thoroughly thawed out, and clad in borrowed clothes, they were served an impossibly large breakfast in the sumptuous dining room. Soon they were joined by Chief Superintendent Morton and another police officer.

"Kathleen! I can't begin to tell you how relieved I am to see you! I ought to be tearing you off a strip, you obstinate little hussy! An absolutely splendid result! We're all so proud of you! Now, some introductions. This is a colleague from Inverness, Duncan Fraser."

"Good morning, sir," said Kathleen politely.

"A very good morning indeed," said Fraser. "Let's not stand on ceremony. Duncan to you, and I'll call you Kathleen, if I may. I'm so pleased to meet you." He then took Dougal warmly by the hand. "Dougal Henderson? Glad to meet you! Tremendous work! The whole thing's wrapped up. We've still to pick up all the lesser Indians, but the Chiefs are accounted for. Makes a refreshing change to catch the head-crooks first, I can tell you!"

"There are, of course, loose ends to be tied up," said Morton "However, they can wait until later. I've laid on transport to get you back to Inverness. You must be dog-tired. Get some sleep and we can pick up the threads again tomorrow. Once again, thanks to you both! You've done a splendid job!"

- - - - - - - - -

The police car sped northwards with Kathleen and Dougal sitting drowsily in the back Suddenly, in all the anticlimax of realising that the whole adventure was over, both felt almost numb with fatigue. At the guest-house, they tumbled into their respective beds and slept until early evening. After a leisurely evening meal, they sauntered along by the river. By the time they returned to the guest-house, they had decided they would announce their engagement just as soon as they could choose a ring when the shops re-opened on Monday. Dougal would then look for a post in the Highlands. Once he was settled, Kathleen and he would marry and live happily ever after!

It did work out something like that. However, Dougal spent a fraught Sunday back on the Insch marshes, trying to help the police recover the body of the late unlamented Bruce. One bit of the peaty bog looked very much like another and locating the right spot proved very difficult. Policemen in inflatable boats probed the depths of the quagmire with long poles, not unlike the procedure for finding casualties of an avalanche. When, at last, they felt sure they had found the right place, a portable pump forced gallons of water from the Spey through a pipe pushed deep down in the mud, creating a muddy brown soup Meanwhile, a second pump sucked the resulting sludge away and fed it back into the river. Eventually, a police diver descended cautiously into the black waters. Working by feel rather than by sight, he managed to attach a line to the corpse. The Thing from the Swamp that they pulled up that day would visit Dougal in nightmares for many nights to come.

Monday, spent with Kathleen, was, by contrast, a wonderful day. The dangers of the past week-end behind them, they planned for a future together. The only slight cloud in Dougal's sky was that he found he still craved excitement and a sense of purpose in life. On Tuesday morning he was reflecting on this as he joined Kathleen for breakfast.

"Hi!," She greeted him. "Sleep well?"

"Great, thanks. What's today's agenda? Had any more thoughts about where we should live?"

"I've just had a phone call from my boss. He and Duncan Fraser want to give us lunch. I have, of course, accepted, which I hope you don't mind. Why is it I think they're up to something?"

"Just that you've got a nasty, suspicious mind." Dougal replied with a grin. "That's what happens when you mix with policemen. You can't take anything at face value, can you?"

"Well, we'll see. Just you wait. Then we'll see."

- - - - - - - - -

Lunch was a delicious meal in lovely surroundings at a hotel at the north end of Loch Ness. As the four settled down with a cafetiere of coffee before them, Duncan said, "Dougal, I believe you're thinking of a move northwards?"

"Yes. Kathleen and I have decided we want to live somewhere in the Highlands, not too far from civilisation, but away from the urban sprawl of the Central Belt."

"Do you know Strathquinnan?"

Dougal did, vaguely. It was a quiet fishing village on the west coast thirty miles or so from Oban. He remembered it as a sheltered anchorage and a pleasant holiday resort. He nodded.

"Well, there's a vacancy there for an English teacher at the High School."

"Aye, and what makes you think I'd get the job if I did apply for it?" asked Dougal with a smile.

"You'll get it. Just get your application in."

"Kathleen, what's going on here?" Kathleen shrugged. Dougal went on, "There's a hidden agenda here, isn't there? Why do you want me at Strathquinnan?"

"Okay, there is. There's something evil going on among teenagers from there. Too many are leaving the community in Strathquinnan and are turning up six months or a year later in one or other of the big cities, either dead or hopeless drug addicts. The source of the problem must be right there in Strathquinnan, but where? On the inside, in daily contact with the kids at school, you might find out something vital that we're missing. Now what do you say?"

Dougal looked at Kathleen then, together, they nodded. With a thrill, Dougal realised he had found that new sense of direction and purpose he wanted so much.

"Good," said Duncan Fraser. "Now that we've got the forgery business behind us, we'll be able to concentrate on this. It's not always that we're able to sew up a case as comprehensively as the Altnariach one. The only remaining mystery is the absence of a stock of completed forged bank-notes. They must be somewhere, but we're baffled."

- - - - - - - - -

There is a family of mice living comfortably in a well-built secure lock-up in Carlisle. Their nest is made of well-chewed, well-forged notes. They are breeding as only mice can, but even so, left in peace, there is ample nesting material to see them and their descendants comfortably through the first half of the 21st Century.